D0863517

DAUGHTERS OF MEMORY

DAUGHTERS
OF
MEMORY

A Story by

PETER NAJARIAN

City Miner ⚒ Books

1986

This book was partially funded with a generous grant from the A.G.B.U. Alex Manoogian Cultural Fund.

Cover painting and illustrations by Peter Najarian
Book Design by David Bullen
Typeset in Mergenthaler Imprint by Harrington-Young
Printed by McNaughton & Gunn

Library of Congress Card Catalogue Number:85-063859
ISBN:0-933944-13-6

First Edition
10 9 8 7 6 5 4 3 2 1 0

For Grandma, who was born around the same time as Picasso and Joyce and who probably starved to death somewhere in the Syrian Desert when Degas died in Paris.

For her and for them and for her young son who would have become an artist had he not died beside her.

For the love of art and for all the kindred souls who share the terror of our history and a love that may redeem it.

For a life devoted to making lines and for that faithful and patient man who once held a child in his lap and showed him pictures and nurtured in his heart the dream of making them. For cousin Archie, Ashod Pinajian.

A Note on the Illustrations:

Soon after this novel was written and many years after thinking that he was unable to draw, the author happened to sit in on an art class given by his friend, Lenny Silverberg, and lo and behold he discovered the wonder and agony of smudging and erasing, (Thank you, Lenny.). This is to remind the reader that the narrator of this story is supposed to be more advanced in his development. For the author himself the knee is still difficult.

In the New Age the Daughters of Memory shall become the Daughters of Inspiration. from *Milton,* by Blake.

All this beauty will follow me throughout my life;/ If my eyes failed, might my hearing last,/ The sound would conjure the gesture she makes. from a poem by Degas when he was going blind.

Whenever or wherever I look, within or without, I always see the Goddess, whose substance is desire, male or female, or in whatever form she is pleased to appear. I see my mother, the crazy girl, beautiful as a sixteen year old, dancing with gentle movements of her body, taking up in turn the flute and the sword, mingling her laughter with her dancing, binding and unbinding her hair as in creation and dissolution. . . . from a Tantrik hymn.

Let me in long draughts taste/ Of the juice of the pomegranate,/ Out of the cup of thy heart/ Quaffing the noblest wine./ After the drinking, bestow the kiss.
from a song to The Heart of Jesus, Hermann Joseph, 12th C.

In the morning after the vision of the grail the castle was empty and desolate. He crossed over the bridge but just barely and the gate almost caught his foot. In the forest on the other side of the river he met an angry woman. 'Perceval!' she said, and this was how he learned his name, for until now he knew himself only as My Dearest Son. 'Perceval,' she said, 'didn't you ask whom the grail is for? Your mother is gone and now you've lost the castle as well.'
adapted from the story of Perceval as told in *The Grail Legend,*
by Emma Jung and Marie-Louise von Franz.

You are all-pervading, eternal and infinitely creative awareness. All else is local and temporary. Don't forget what you are. . . . A person is but the sum total of memories. . . . I ask you only to stop imagining that you were born, have a mother, will die, and so on. Just try, make a beginning—it's not as hard as you think. . . . As long as you are enmeshed in a particular personality you can see nothing beyond it. But as a tiny point of a pencil can draw innumerable pictures so does the dimensionless point of awareness draw the contents of the vast universe. Find that point and be free. Find what you have never lost, find the inalienable. from *I Am That,* conversations with Nisargadatta.

DAUGHTERS OF MEMORY

The Old Grapevine

Lines upon lines, they flow like food for the tail-eating snake. They love the void and they grow in death, they rise and become part of it like murals on a cracking wall that become the cracks themselves.

Dear Death, dear dying friends, here are more of them, another mystery and a search. The plot is simple: an old hairy-nosed and horny artist is reviewing his life's work and he confronts the spirit of history, of our species who kill each other and of his grandmother who was slaughtered in the desert.

Who is she, what does she look like? He wants to paint her as if she is the woman he's always wanted and the quest for her figure leads him through the labyrinth of the mysterious female.

Meanwhile life goes on. A bunch of old Armenian women are sitting around in a place like Fresno, California, and the grapevines are like those they once knew in Turkey. They were youngsters in Turkey when the Armenians were massacred and like other survivors they came to America and settled in a town across the river from New York. They worked in factories and raised families and when they retired they moved near a vineyard where they get together every once in a while and shoot the bull.

Our hero's mother could be one of them. He visits her about once a month and she tells him of her own mother whose face she can't remember. He struggles to imagine that face as if it were the image of a home they both lost in their different ways. He tries to find her inside himself but his imagination fails, his memories interfere and they become like veils he can't clear away.

Back in his shack in Berkeley he tries to figure them out and they grow like doodles in a margin of a letter. Some of these letters are to his old friend, Charlie, whom he never sees anymore. The lines twist and curve like an old grapevine at the end of harvest, the shredded bark and tortured trunk like an old ego on a cross, its arms out as if it were praying for death

By a Vineyard in the Great Valley of the West

The harvest is over, the summer is gone, and yet more grapes still hang on the hairy vine, their soft skin now freckled brown and their juice very sweet.

They survive, they ripen, and as they dry they grow even sweeter.

A fat moon appears above the horizon and the long rays of the sundown send blue and purple shadows to some ancient figures bathed in gold. One of them pinches the air and shakes it back and forth.

· Eh?
· Don't ask me, I never knew that kind of love.
· I watch it on my television story.
· I don't watch that garbage anymore.
· They should tell it to the toilet and pull the handle.
· No, I like it, it's just like life.
· Whose life?
· Not mine.
· Which one of us knew that kind of romance?
· Don't look at me. In the orphanage I said okay as long as he was not crippled or blind, so they showed me a picture of a soldier with a hat in his arm. But when he came to get me on Ellis Island his one eye was glass and he was lame from a wound in the war. And as if that was not enough he was sixteen years older than I and I was not even sixteen.
· But you loved him.
· I learned to love him but he was not my sweetheart.
· What about Anna, she had a sweetheart?
· Her sweetheart was a Moslem.
· She was in love with the boy next door.
· A Moslem.
· Moslems like Christian girls.
· Those filth.
· Moslem or Christian they had a son.
· A bastard.
· A bastard to you, to her a prince.
· You remember Jack-knife Nishan, his sister-in-law had one of those

bastards. No one talked with her when she walked down the street with it. Some even spit at it.

· No one spit at Anna because no one knew.

· I never knew till you told me.

· Tell us again.

· Her husband died not even a year after the baby was born and that very year the massacre started. She was living with his family and her father and brothers came to get her. 'No,' she said, 'how can I leave my child?' 'Your child is a Moslem bastard,' they said, 'you're coming with us.'

· She should have taken the child.

· Her husband's family would have killed her.

· Poor girl.

· Girl is right, no woman would leave her child.

· Her father was a powerful man and he took her away whether she wanted to go or not.

· Either that or become a Moslem.

· I know more than one who did.

· They're still over there.

· No, Anna left her son and went to Aleppo with her father. First to Aleppo and then to Alexandria and her father died in Alexandria.

· Then she tried to go back to her son.

· No, she came here. In Alexandria she met Yero Topjian. You know Yero Topjian, Asniv's sister-in-law's husband.

· Asniv, the duck-killer's daughter?

· That's right. Yero married her sister-in-law. Anyway, he was in Alexandria after the war and he brought Anna here to marry his cousin, Levon.

· Levon whose nephew married Halvah Harry's daughter.

· That's right. Levon was her husband's uncle. He married Anna and took her to Watertown.

· My brother-in-law lived in Watertown fifty years ago.

· I remember going to Watertown by boat.

· How could you go to Watertown by boat?

· In those days we used to go from New York to Boston by boat. I think the dock was at Chelsea. Wasn't the dock at Chelsea?

· Who cares about Chelsea? What happened to Anna?

· Did she have another child?

· No, she never had another child.

· The Moselm was her curse.

· Curse or not she stayed with Levon and they had a grocery shop. They worked hard and saved their money and around her neck she wore a locket of her baby's hair and no one ever knew.

· Poor woman.

· Not so poor, she had a house and they lived well.

· But she had no child.

· She had a child. Somewhere back there she had a child.

· That was her suffering.

· Each of us had our suffering.

· That was her suffering but not her child's. She lost hope but he didn't. 'Who is my mother,' he kept asking, 'where did she go?'

· Good for him.

· Yes, he looked for his mother. He went to Aleppo, he went to Alexandria, and in Alexandria he found her address in Watertown.

· *Vai, vai,* the little Moslem bastard.

· How happy she must have been.

· She could not read the letter fast enough. 'I am your son,' he wrote, 'I want to see you.'

· I saw something like this on my television story. It was about a girl who gave her child away for adoption.

· Our people don't give our children away for adoptions.

· Oh no?

· Anna did not give her child away. She lost him and now she found him.

· She found him, yes, but Levon also read the letter.

· Uh-oh.

· 'What's this?' he says. 'What's it look like?' she says. 'It's from my son. I'm going to see him.' 'You're not doing anything,' he says, 'you're not going near that Moslem bastard.'

· He's jealous.

· He's not jealous, he's furious.

· His whole family was killed by them.

· That was the past and she had suffered enough. 'Do you think,' she says to him, 'that you can stop me?'

· How can he stop her? Who is more important, a husband or a son?

· Sometimes a husband is too strong.

· No husband could be strong enough for Anna. 'Stay out of my way,' she says, 'or you'll never see me again.'

· Good for her.

· 'Don't bring him back here,' Levon said, 'no Moslem bastard is going
to step in this house.'

· He was ashamed.

· Let him be ashamed. Love is more important than shame.

· Not in those days. In those days shame was everything.

· That's because everyone was so close. You couldn't go to the toilet
without someone knowing.

· And now everyone was going to know about Anna.

· Let them know. She had money of her own and she flew to Beirut
and her son met her there.

· Mother and son together after all those years.

· Just like my television story.

· Is her son here now?

· No, he couldn't leave his life back there but he comes to see her once
a year.

· Once a year, big deal.

· At least she sees him once a year. Some mothers never see their sons.

· Some sons don't love their mothers.

· How could a son not love his mother?

The Model, The Whore, and the Old Tom Cat

The lines sprawl and return to the center. Who is the figure buried
inside them?

One night the model was so lovely I wanted to fuck her on the platform. I who, who are these eyes and their unending hunger?

She lay with her legs open and her face in her hand and when a line approached her mound she was not a model anymore, she was a lovely young woman naked on a batik shawl.

'*I paint with my prick,*' Renoir said, his crumpled body in a wheelchair and the brush wadded between his twisted fingers, the great nudes rising above him.

Should our hero be any different? He too wanted to squeeze her buttocks and suck her breasts as if she were an apple. But she was not an apple. An apple doesn't stare back and when she stared back her own eyes seemed to come from another world. I am a woman, they said, I am not a form you can fuck with lines.

Line by line to the curl of her navel and the darkness of her bush, the pencil lingering to draw each hair, hair by hair for another figure who keeps staring back.

She slipped into her robe and walked around the room. She nodded with a smile, her breasts showing through the satin.

'Nice drawing.'

'Thanks.'

'I like the way you caught my pose.'

'It's a good pose.'

She lay down again, her body so familiar she seemed eternal, the same old knee that used to be so difficult, the same curves into her labia. She could disappear and still be drawn from memory. '*Muscles I know,*' said the master Ingres, '*they are my friends, but I've forgotten their names.*'

She dressed in the other room and left with her bicycle, her own desire pedalling into her future, all the sketches left behind like petals in her wake, another nude buried with all the others, all the years of wanting her and old enough now to be her father.

Older than Gauguin when he fled to the Pacific. Older than Lautrec when he drank himself to death. Older than Van Gogh when he ate paint and shot himself. '*Keep painting,*' he wrote to a friend, '*and visit a whore every two weeks.*'

Déhanchement on the corner.

'Hi, you wanna date?'

'Sure, how much is it?'

'How much you want?'

'Whatever you have.'

'A blowjob and a fuck?'

'Sure, what else is there?'

'Anything else is extra.'

'No, I don't need extras.'

'Then, it's thirty-five for me and ten for the room.'

Enough for how much canvas? How many nudes for her hot pants and fauve lipstick?

'Come here by the sink and let me wash you.'

Her hands gentle on the throbbing while she talked about her charm bracelet, each charm a symbol and a memory.

'And real gold.'

Cynthia. Two children by caeserian and a scar across her belly, her flesh warm and familiar. But her client was tense and his cock was soft.

'Relax and let me have it.'

And she put it in her mouth as if with love.

'You're nice, no, I really mean it, what's your sign?'

He was hard now and he crouched above her. Then he paused.

'Comon now, don't be shy.'

And she drew him in as if she were a wife.

'See, you're not as old as you think.'

But she was neither wife nor lover and she would not kiss. Somewhere inside her a door was closed and he spilled into a darkness that could never be pregnant.

And yet he held on and tried to stay in as long as he could.

She waited and then eased from under the burden.

She yawned as she dressed.

'Are you tired?'

'Am I tired. But I'm goin out one more time and it's home to bed for little Cindy.'

She wrote her number on a matchbook and tapped him gently on the shoulder.

'Well, Zeke, I hope I see you again. Don't you forget me now, you hear?

She scumbles with all the others, her gesture buried in the huge pile, all the figures like leaves for compost or mulch.

Where is the center, the buried seed?

The cat curls on the dictionary, the leaves of the prayer plant are furled asleep, the refrigerator stops moaning.

Where is the end of desire, where is release?

In the revelation of dawn comes the wail of the old tom cat crouching under the bamboo bush, his mutilated ear and funny face so vivid in the new light of the red sky. He keeps trying. He keeps wandering the neighborhoods and spraying his need like frescoes to a god.

I don't give it up, he wails, my need is my nature.

He stares back at the homo sapien in sweatshirt and corduroys, the old fugitive of the humane society.

Come, he wails, come join my caterwaul of the ages, the search for the one inside.

The Lag-Lag

· Tell me the truth, do I smell of piss?

· No, not so far.

· Thank goodness. I used to smell it on Agavni before she died. I wanted to tell her but I didn't want to hurt her feelings.

· I used to smell it too. She used to wash her underwear every day but it was not enough.

· I go through twenty pair of underwear a week. Good thing I have a drier, what would my neighbors think if they saw all them on the line?

· Well thank God you can still wash them yourself.

· You said it, I'd rather leak piss in my own house than wear a diaper in one of those others.

· My children say they'll never let me go to one of those places.

· They all say that.

· I never heard of those places when I was young.

· Whoever started them, let the dog shit in his father's mouth.

· They're not so bad.

· They stink and you know it.

· Everywhere stinks if your ass is shitty.

· Just like the lag-lag.

· What lag-lag?

· The lag-lag with the shitty ass. Everytime he'd fly to a lake he would say, 'It stinks here.' And everywhere he went would stink because he would stink.

· Let's talk about something else.

· Bring some pumpkin seeds. I want to do something else with my mouth.

· No, we must keep talking. Talking is good for us, no matter what we talk about.

She Goes All The Way Back

Whoever she is she goes all the way back in all the dreams of water and flying.

She was in the vision on the way home from kindergarten by the

park, the shiny horsechestnuts falling on the sidewalk like jewels
bursting from their hoary shells. She was the little girl who disappeared in the green.

She appeared again in the blaze of adolescence, her face by the window and the hair in her armpits moist and silken. '*I love you*,' someone had scribbled in her notebook, and she flushed it down the hole of
all things secret. She knew what those words meant, they meant *sex*,
whatever that meant.

Where did she go, when would she say yes? The road opened with
six hundred dollars and a heavy duffle full of paper, the blue hills
leading to Mexico as if she would be waiting with a mango by her
breast.

But she was not there. Nor in England or India and the years passed
like pages of an atlas, a postcard every week to an old woman who sits
under a lamp and asks how come she was never found.

'I don't know, Ma. Maybe I was afraid of women.'

She stares into her sewing and remembers a remedy from the old
days.

'I once heard that a good cure for fear is to drink a little of your own
urine.'

Ma. Always Ma. Who looms over the question with hands like a
butcher's and the legs of a fullback, her grip relentless with mounds of
dough, her arms full of laundry. The beloved Ma a son yells at in his
dreams.

But she was not to blame. The old woman who sometimes pisses in
her pants when she laughs too hard is not the harlot-angel across the
continents. There is no need to run from her anymore whose arms the
lost youth ripped away in the name of adventure, her voice pathetic
through the phone in that first cockroach hallway of artisthood.

'Doon chebedekas? *Aren't you coming home this weekend?*'

'*No.*'

'*Why not?*'

'*I don't want to.*'

'*No reason?*'

'*No, I just don't want to.*'

She never asked again and stayed behind on the long road of laun-
dromats and hot plates, her clean sheets and jars of food always waiting.

Smiling, always smiling, as if wagging her tail like a samoyed dog so happy to see her master, her shaggy white hair winnowed by the years and her chamois face like a map of her life, her milky eyes in the folding lids of an Asian quiet.

She moves with the grace of an elephant. She sways her giant buttocks from her kitchen to her garden and back again, a mini Demeter wearing old man slippers and a loud mu-mu, her body opulent in a steamy bath.

'Will you rub my back for me, my son?'

Hot and pink beneath the flaxen cloth, massive like the flank of a beautiful animal. Not a vision but the vegetable wonder whose stubble mustache and garlic breath a pubescent boy once felt ashamed of.

A female of the specie, her huge breasts a reminder that she was not always the one who panics at a traffic signal.

In an old brown photograph of her youth she poses like a princess with her hand on her hip and her left foot forward, a sexy gap between her teeth and her toes curling above a glass shoe. She was one of them, a model for the figure who never comes clear.

Worms

· I made *bastarmah* and left it in the garage and it got worms in it.
· Where did you buy the meat?
· It wasn't the meat, the garage was too damp.
· You don't know, it could be the meat.
· How could it be the meat, I soaked it in salt for three days.
· The meat nowdays is safe, it's not like the old days.
· I hope so, I still remember that worm I pulled out of my ass.
· What worm?
· I never told you about the worm I pulled out of my ass?
· Would I forget something like that?
· It was when I first came to this country. I was sitting on the toilet and
  I felt something down below so I reached there and pulled it out. But
  it had no end, I just kept pulling and pulling.
· The head was still inside you.
· That's right, that's what Knucklebones the country doctor said. He
  told me to eat nothing but raw pumpkin seeds for three days and
  then drink castor oil. So I did that and the head came out and I never
  had one since.
· I never had one of those kind, I had the long pink kind.
· Oh, I had one of those too.
· I never had any, thank goodness.
· They're just worms, they have to live, too.

Dear Charlie

What do you look like now? Are your ears hairy? Do you trim your
eyebrows?

   In the dream this morning your hair was falling over your eyes like
it used to when we were kids, your smile full of those great buck teeth
before they straightened out. I hugged and kissed you and we were
pals again.

   Here now in these little snapshots your hair is wavy and you wear
that big shit-eating grin like a young wop about to conquer America,
the son of Hemingway in love with words, a book always in the pocket
of your fatigue jacket.

All of us together like warriors in the lull of battle.

Leo like a hood with his collar up and his shoulders high.

Tony the tough guy with his arms crossed and his shirtsleeves rolled to his biceps.

Shlomo with his first goatee and a Pall Mall dangling from his big lips.

And here by the bench in Washington Park, you and Dolores and me in between, our arms around each other like guerillas after a victory.

Snap, snap, snap, how heroic we were.

We survived, we did not die, Leo who joined the reserves instead of getting drafted, Tony who had that bad knee from football, Shlomo who pretended to be a homosexual and Zeke who said he shot heroin and you who were deferred because you were going to have a child.

But we would have been too early for Vietnam, the Village still a place where we could afford a pad, the basements full of action painting and amazing jazz, the big paperbacks just starting to get printed and each new edition like a fresh comic. How many did we stuff in our pants and then bury like treasure in our flophouse rooms?

Where are they now, where is that little copy of Rimbaud and that Coltrane album with his picture on the cover, where are all the sketches and poems of our passionate youth, what flowers or fungi will they feed with the compost of our past, the marijuana with the shades down, the cactus buds from a cactus ranch in Texas—Smith's Cactus Ranch, wasn't that it's name? When they arrived they were soft and moldy and we had to eat them with pints of ice-cream and peaches.

We never stopped eating. We ate hot rolls from the back of a bakery at three in the morning and we walked across the bridge at dawn. Once we walked all the way to new Guggenheim, we never stopped walking and talking about art.

We read of Cezanne and Zola growing up together and never seeing each other again. We read of Lenin taking Trotsky for a tour around London when they still had time to screw around. We read of Freud walking with Rilke in a beautiful meadow and Freud remembering how sad Rilke was from so much beauty. We never stopped reading about writers and artists and we wanted someone to write about us and how we waved our arms and got excited and waited for Dolores to serve the pasta.

She would fall asleep with the light on while we stayed up and made more mess, Leo and Tony arguing about God and Shlomo sprinkling beer on their heads, Leo pontificating with his finger in the air like Socrates on his deathbed and you smoking all those Chesterfields, all our words reduced to silliness by her bulging navel.

'We're born and we die and there's just sixty or seventy years in between that we got to fill up.'

'Fuck you, Leo, you're dying, not me.'

Snap, snap, snap of the little Brownie like swipes of a grim reaper, each photo like a flower of perennials decapitated in the red leaves, our figures like ghosts in the negatives held to the light.

We will each die so far from the other.

You playing that Ma Rainey record all the time.

Shlomo going to Brooklyn to score some grass.

Leo and Tony hitchhiking back and forth to New Brunswick.

The march for Chessman, the struggle in the south, the committee for nuclear disarmament even way back then.

The year 1960 of the Christian calendar, the history of the universe in a few snapshots of our ignorant youth, Dolores staring back.

Who is she, not your former wife and the young woman your best friend betrayed you for, but the blurry image with a strange smile, the pregnant Mona Lisa in a tattered raincoat, the mystery woman of our nightmare past?

The Garbage Man

· I'd like to get a job in one of those hamburger places.
· She's got more money than a pasha and now she wants to be a servant.
· You don't even know how to write. How are you going to write the orders?
· I don't have to work in the front, I can work in the back. I can wash dishes.
· They're not going to hire someone your age.
· This isn't the village. Old people don't work in this country. Young people can't even find work.
· Diamond Ring Zakar owns some of those places. Maybe he can give you a job.
· I wouldn't work for Diamond Ring if I were you.
· He's not an easy boss.
· He was a slave himself when he was a child.
· Was he one too?
· His mother left him under a tree before she was slaughtered. Some Kurds got him and made him a slave. He lived with them for some years before he escaped.
· He's a good boy. He can't help it if he loves money.
· So what good did it to him? He waited till he was fifty to marry and then to one who couldn't have a child.
· I wonder who he'll leave his money to?
· The government will get it.
· Let them have it, they were good to him.
· Why should they get it? They don't know how to use it.
· I don't care what happens to it, just don't give any to me. I have enough trouble giving away what I have.
· Then why do you want to make more?
· It's not for the money.
· She wants to be around young people.
· Young people don't want to be around us.
· They think we have some kind of disease.
· My garbage man is young and he always stops for a cup of coffee in my garage.
· In your garage?

· Why sure, didn't you know my garage is a coffee house?

· That was a good idea putting a stove in your garage.

· Why sure, who wants to sit in the house? I pull the door up and I'm open to the street.

· That's what everyone does on my street. They live in the garage all the time.

· I wouldn't be able to talk to my garbage man if I was inside. I give him coffee and *chor-eg* whenever he comes. He's good to me. He takes all my garbage no matter how much I have.

The Beautiful Woman and The Scummy Waves

In the supermarket the other day the cashier looked just like Dolores at that age, the same dimples in her smile. 'Hey, I know you,' thought the horny old geezer with the tofu and catfood, 'I know that smile, I used to adore you.'

Everyone adored her but no one more than her husband and his friend, the two of them shopping together to buy her gifts. For she was the beautiful young woman, that human flower behind all songs and tragedies, or rather she wore that flower in her turn and passed it on before she ever became aware of it. She wore it in her hips she thought were too wide and in her nose she thought was too big, but most of all she wore it in her smile she could never hide and it seemed to come from that realm so contrary to pornos and beauty contests. It was everywhere in any supermarket and no one had to peek inside a centerfold to feel its power. It grew inside her innocence and blossomed despite her shame and not until she saw it wither and die would she realize where it came from, the deep lustre of her hair and the smoothness of her flesh like a glow only others could feel while she herself suffered her own kind of fear and ignorance.

One morning on her way to work in St. Vincent's Hospital she passed the old House of Detention for Women and there were some young men on the sidewalk. It's not there anymore, it was torn down and there's supposed to be a library in its place, but in those days it towered in the middle of Sixth Avenue and as the young Hispanics stood in the snow and yelled up to their sweethearts in the windows above she stood and listened to them. 'Zeke,' she would say later, 'there they were yelling 'Maria!' and 'Consuela!' and I felt so sad for those poor girls up there in the middle of the city looking down at the rest of us.' And when she spoke of that moment her voice had a special kind of sympathy as if she herself were locked away for some petty crime like being a young woman who looked in the mirror too much.

She was so fearful of her image she could be devastated by the slightest finger pointing at her mistakes. She stayed in a shadow whenever she could and felt most comfortable cooking and cleaning while the boys showed off.

Nothing was more important to them than her beauty and yet they would talk about other things like art and god. They would go by the river and study the play of sunspecks on the scummy waves. They would stand on the pier and plan their route on the next voyage through poverty and struggle, two little immigrants from the same childhood, a bundle of dreams on their shoulders for another shore. They threw pebbles into the waves and looked across the river to where they were born, and one of them turned to the other and said, 'Find a woman, Zeke. It hurts me to see you alone so much.'

Where Was Your Mother Buried?

· I don't know where my mother was buried.
· My mother was buried in a ditch outside Damascus.
· I don't know where my mother was buried but I know where her brother died. He went to Soviet Armenia and then he starved to death.
· I remember my mother a little. I remember she used to hit me a lot.
· She must have been a young mother.
· I remember my father saying, 'You hit a donkey when it doesn't move but you don't have to hit a child.'
· I wish I could remember my mother. I wish I knew what she looked like.
· She didn't look like us, I'll tell you that. She was too young to look like us.

The Eighty-Year Old Child

She flutters her fingers and waves bye-bye.

Will she be there again next month?

She will die before the birch tree she planted in her yard. Her body, voice and touch will become the soil she plays with every day, her bee-stings and muddy fingers finally joining the mother she lost in the desert.

She never stays still.

'Ma, I can't draw you if you don't sit still.'

'Draw me from memory.'

She embraces her grapevine and her pomegranate. Her lemon, rose, and olive. Her fava bean, strawberry, okra, and apricot. Her fig, zucchini, asparagus and melon. Her nectarine, orange, grapefruit and peach. Her quince, eggplant, stringbean and tomato. Her fifty years in the factory buried in the compost so that now she can work not for money anymore but because what else is there to do more joyful? Is she not her mother's daughter?

Little Siranoush alone now in the great valley. In her own house with wall to wall synthetic fiber and all the heat and hot water she wants for the rest of her life.

'What do you have for me,' she asks the young mailman in his short pants and long socks, 'bills or checks?'

Infected with her smile he greets her good day and hands her the blue check from the government. The white one from the union will come in a few days. They are more than enough since she still eats like a peasant and remains invulnerable to American more-more. Here now in the home she bought with nickel bargains and pinch-penny discounts, the former hawkeye of the avenue who couldn't read but could spot a mistake in any scale or addition, all the years of a dollar here and a dollar there paying off with cash down for her own place in a maze of stucco tickytacks.

Siranoush the householder, Heritage Model Homes. Acres and acres of fruit trees bulldozed and paved in the name of profit. She replants a few of them and who will deny her this last home amid the rampant greed and ignorance? In the old days she would have been crowded with her daughter-in-law in a coldwater flat. Maybe in another life she will have a home and a family as well.

'But you can't have everything in this one. Everyone wants everything and happiness too. You know what happiness is? It is this piece
of bread and going to the toilet by myself.'

She made it. And lived long enough to enjoy the benefits of evolu-
tion. The shopping center is nearby and even her bank is coming
soon. The bus is only a quarter and the utilities give her a refund every
year.'

'They give it to me,' she says with her big tits, 'because I'm a *seen-
yirr citizen*. What does *seen-yirr* mean, my son?'

She spreads her huge thighs and bends to her weeds. She stands
back and studies her leaves. She's been out there since six this morning and it's time to break for lunch, a *boreg* of fried weed and leftover
dough. And now her story comes on, *The Young and The Restless*.
The scripts are trite enough for her to follow and she doesn't need to
understand most of the words.

'It's always the same story over and over.'

Here now in the present she has landed on like a coconut from
across the ocean, her bumpy shell bobbing on the waves of history, her
voyage tossed steerage class through sickness and poverty, her survival washed ashore into dry weather and sunshine all the time. And
here may her shell crack, dessicate and shred in a gentle breeze, the
white seed spill sweet milk and die glorious. May she never again eat
garbage from the gutter.

One morning she was still sleeping when her son woke up. Her
bedroom door was open and she sprawled with her legs apart, the
hem of her nightgown curled around her wrinkled thighs. She was so
still she looked like a corpse and he loved her so deeply he was filled
with dread. He often imagined her dead as if to prepare himself for
the day he would come to this house and she would be gone. And yet
the older she grew the more alive she seemed, or rather he was growing
and his love deepening so that year by year she was becoming less a
mother than a child, a little girl he could see clearer and clearer beneath the wrinkles and the cataracts. He loved her so deeply he began
to cry. Why? Why did love always make him cry as if it always opened
the door to being alone and the beloved so far away? She seemd so far
away and then suddenly she started to snore and he was okay again.
She was back in the room with her nose in the air and her mouth
open, her arms out and her blunt fingers pendulant in a ballet gesture. He wanted to draw her but knew that like his cats she would

never stay still. And she moved and hugged the pillow and he wished he could slip inside her dream, the little girl with no one but the universe for nurture. Snoring. Dreaming of the dead, the face of her own mother too deep to recall.

The One Too Deep To Be Recalled

'What do you remember, Ma?'

'I remember many things but I can't remember my mother's face.'

'Tell me what you remember.'

'I remember in the winter we lived in town and she made bread in a small clay stove with a wood fire. It was outside in the courtyard where all the women baked in turn. I remember the circles of dough were rolled flat and baked into bubbling wafers and afterwards they poured the ashes into a barrel of water and let it stand overnight. With that detergent of ashen water they soaked their laundry the next morning and then smacked it with heavy sticks on a stone table by the fountain. She would have my little brother at her feet and my older brother would be off somewhere drawing. He used to draw all the time and when we lived in town my father worked for a butcher. We were peasants but we always had enough to eat. On Sundays she always made *kuftah*. Most of the families made *kuftah* on Sundays just like the Italians in our old neighborhood used to make spaghetti sauce on the weekends. She would pound the meat with a mallet and through the window you could hear the knock-knock-knock of the other women pounding around the yard. We ate and slept in that one room. We sat on the floor and when night came we cleared the floor and unfolded the blankets and used the heavy quilts for mattresses. Once I heard her and my father make sounds in the night. My father was a gentle man but she was robust and strong. Her face however I can't remember at all.'

Mother of mother in the desert of oblivion, magna mater in a tattered calico.

Grandma called Vartanoush, Sweet Rose in sfumato.

She lies buried like an ancient figure in a peeling wall, the void of her face filled with all the women loved and slaughtered in their turn, a madonna with a son.

'My older brother's name was Arshag. I remember he used to sit by the window. There was only one window in our room in town and he used to sit by it and draw all the time. Sometimes I look at the young man who reads the news on the television and his face seems to remind me of my brother even though my brother was only about twelve. I look and look and try to bring back my brother's face but I can't. I can't remember  his face but I remember once he was angry with me when I broke his pencil. He held me by the arm and said, 'If you tell me the truth I won't hit you but if you lie I will.' And I said, 'Yes, I broke your pencil.' I never forget that. I can't remember his face but his words are still clear.'

Uncle Arshag, the peasant boy in love with drawing. The little Giotto scratching sheep on a rock. The little Daumier sneaking sketches when his boss was gone. What would he have painted had he lived?

His bones become chalk and his blood a pigment, he and his mother in a primed canvas, their death the stare of its emptiness.

'In the spring we went to our acre and I remember the bridge we had to cross to get there. I remember riding in a cart behind the donkey and the long road out of the city. Every spring we went to our acre and we stayed there until the winter.'

The mud dries fast in the rising sun, the fields splashed with mustard and the hills rich with the sap green of the new grass. She begins to emerge with lupine and poppies, a plot of earth and a bundle of seeds.

She is the lost one, the earth her grandson longs to embrace, the young peasant woman who would bring him home again. She is the generous water and friendly light he struggles to touch with all his lines.

'We slept outside on a platform built on poles above the ground and the donkey slept nearby. There was never any rain and my mother cooked on a small fire with hot stones. Yes, of course, vegetables and bulghur, what else? Yes, just like camping, we camped out for half the year.'

The cobalt night fills with stars, alizarin crimson and some tea for the dawn, Claude and Corot and the pastorals of Tolstoi, the hard work rewarded not by money but the abundant grapes like jewels from the sun.

'She stomped the grapes in burlap and then boiled them into syrup, I remember she poured the syrup into heavy jars and then sealed the jars with mud and fig leaves. Some of the syrup she poured over sheets and dried into *bastik* and with the *bastik* and the syrup my father could barter for wheat. She boiled the wheat and then dried it. I remember going with my father to get it ground into bulghur. I remember the sagging neck of the ox that turned the wheel.'

Each day a different chore, the clothes pounded in the stream, the milk from the neighbor's cow strained into cheese or swung into butter, the wool spun or knitted or beaten with the forked branch and then aired in the sun and quilted into blankets. She is the simple life of strong hands and many cousins, all the peasants sketched and studied across the continents, her back bent under a load like that young woman in Nepal who climbed barefoot up the trail with her huge bundle of wood, her heels cracked and petrified like a cave painting.

She stands in the copper light of the sundown and rests a moment with her donkey. She picks a beggar's lice from his warm head. His adorable eyes are like the hills, the soft neutral witness to her labor and her love. She hugs him, his earthy breath warm on her face.

A small family has sprouted in the corner of the universe. Of all the infinite seeds that fly across the void a few survive and germinate, their tiny leaves twinkling in the mound. The acre glows like a miracle, the horizon like gold leaf behind her purple silhouette.

But what is that cloud like a gash in the sky? It deepens into a bloody red.

What disease or beast will grind her into the garden she nurtures? The sky now darkens from red to black and the pastoral becomes a nightmare.

She writhes, she withers, she stares back through barbed wire and floodlights, the canvas swirling in the filth of precious metals.

Who is she, what is the face that always fades into history, her portrait always glazed with the women of memory, the young woman on the steps of a bank in Calcutta with her little daughter picking lice from her matted hair, the young Mexican with rotten teeth and tabid lungs, the sad Arab in a whorehouse in Casablanca with her legs open and her labia like rose-petals in her black bush?

Arak

· I dreamt of my husband last night.
· Was it a sex dream?
· Not really. We just hugged and kissed.
· Did he give you something? It's good if the dead give you something but it's bad if they take something away.
· We just kissed.
· How old was he?
· He was young.
· How old were you?
· I guess I was young too.

· He was a good boy. He could have lived a little longer.
· He drank too much.
· No, he didn't.
· But he liked his *arak*.
· They all liked their *arak*.
· That's because it was Zevart's *arak*. She was the best bootlegger around.
· Her whole house used to stink every harvest time. The Italians would be making wine and she would be soaking raisins and that whole house used to stink like Secaucus.
· Secaucus doesn't stink anymore, at least that's what they say.
· How would anyone know? Everybody's gone.

Alchemy

Burnt almond shells for black, garlic for mordant, chickenbones for size, in the old days a painting was a compost and we now struggle to preserve it.

And yet how we loved our fugitive colors and the sketches we doodled on decaying paper.

Where is the one of Nelly that year in London? Where is Nelly herself and her curiosity and her humor, her sweaters and her cunt, a hardon rising even before she undressed? Where does a smile go when a person dies?

She would always laugh when she got into bed and slipped under the eiderdown.

'You put the cup in, Zeke.'

The flexible ring would wriggle through her labia like a rubber moon of death, all our children suffocating in our slobbering wrestle and her Liverpool accent.

'Fuck me, Zekus.'

'Okay, Nelly.'

'Zeke?'

'What?'

'How many times do you think you can?'

'I don't know.'

'Let's try for as many times as we can.'

Hunger pent in the genitals and a phallus always ready, only youth can could know those successive erections.

'Let's try for six.'

'No, that was the last one.'

'Oh do let us try again, Zeke, let's try another pose.'

Youth spent in the blaze of discovery, buried and bound with the shroud of pleasure, she tasted so good. She would turn on her side and whisper silly jokes, her hair fragrant in the calm while her lover cupped her tit in gratitude, his wrinkled genitals glued to her buttocks like a quiet pachyderm.

Hold on to her, they said, don't let her go, the fear of her leaving like a wind that would drive her away.

'But Zeke, you don't love me.'

'Why do you say that? I do love you.'

'No, you don't love me, you love your apples.'

Where is she now, the mother of the child the appleman never had? Here now in memory she sits by the window in her kitchen on Finchley Road, her hand in her cheek and her lip turned in that insouciant pose she always liked to affect.

What are the lines for the taste of her nipples, what are the colors for the smell of her neck, her clothes bursting from her closet and her checks always bouncing, the vain and cheerful female always out for a good time?

She came like a water bird that winter by the docks and by summer she was off somewhere looking for a nest. She wouldn't reappear until years later when she was bald and shrivelled in a hospital ward. 'What I really miss,' she told a friend, 'is making love with a man.'

Lapis for blue, metal and earth for red and yellow, they never die. Dear Nelly, dear death, somewhere inside them moves the secret for making you smile again.

Rose Juice

· There's a sale on tombstones in the marble place downtown.
· Business is slow. People want to be burned nowadays.
· It's the new style.
· They feed your ashes to the fish.
· No, I want a place in the earth.
· I already have one. I bought it cheap last year.
· Aren't you going to lie with your husband?
· No one's left back there. All my family's here now.
· My grandchild says it's a waste of space. He wants the graveyard to be a park.
· I don't mind children playing over me.
· I don't mind children playing over me but I get upset when they play over my flowers.
· You should have roses, they won't play by a rose bush.
· I have enough roses in the back.
· Did you make jelly from the petals?
· No, my family likes the syrup better. My grandchildren love it. They don't want soda, they said, they want rose juice.

The Vision

She appeared as if through a veil in that first wet dream, a pubescent girl whose glow brightened as she approached. *Come,* she said, *come closer,* and in her arms a light suddenly streamed up the spine and flowered behind the eyes, the sun bursting through the alley in the daze of awakening, the genitals calm and glutinous.

Where did she go? Who was she, her hair tawny like the dreamer's and her face somehow familiar as if she were a sister who would bring him home again?

Then a mother came in to make the bed. She puffed the pillow and swept the sheet with her hand and saw the spot of wet in the center. She pulled the sheet away and returned with a square of old flannel and placed it on the mattress and then covered it with a fresh sheet.

She didn't want the mattress to be stained and on the flannel the stains began to overlap like signatures from the deep, the girl becoming a woman as the dreamer became a man, but never again would she have that glow.

Instead it passes from dreams to moments in the swift and fleeing realm he could enter only by unawares, the sudden flash of a teenager on a bus or of that young woman on a paper-route who came out in her kimono to get the milk by the door and her breast suddenly naked as she bent forward in the veil of dawn.

And not only of women but of the algae on an old tugboat or the gulls by the dock, of the palisades rising like gods by the waterfront or the clouds rolling above the city, of the grass one afternoon in football practice while the coaches were busy with the rest of the team and the cheerleaders were practicing by the bleachers, the sky suddenly opening and the autumn clouds glowing in the aftermath of rain, the soiled jersies glowing across the field in the soft rainbow colors of a waning light, a deep silence suddenly throbbing with the rich colors of the turf and the sweat from the helmet, a mysterious love rising with tears and mixing in a boy's heart with a grief he couldn't fathom.

Who was it for, who was she who always disappeared?

I will be an artist, he decided. Someday I will paint that glow and find her whoever she is who lives inside it.

And the years passed like the fugitive colors of the rose in the clouds, the vision always fading and the lines flowing to a vanishing point. Where is that point where the I may also vanish, the end of longing and despair?

It always opens to a new landscape, the horizon a woman and the path like a furrow through her loins. Here now by the water the clouds glaze the sky into crimson and mauve and become mirrored by the shore until both shore and sky seem like halves of her giant vulva, the black waves like a crease between her labia, a flock of gulls standing quietly like vultures at the sun's death.

She always seems to appear at sundown or just before the glow of dawn disappears into light. She seems more the glow itself than any figure it could silhouette.

Come, she seems to say, *come closer*, as if she is standing in an old abandoned farm with a donkey by her side, the field full of wild poppies and the old farmtools like sacred relics from an ancient temple.

The Donkey

"Do you remember the donkey, Ma?"

"I remember the donkey as well as my mother. I can remember sitting on that donkey many times. Maybe I loved the donkey more than her, I can't remember loving her, I was too young to love her, but to this day I've loved donkeys."

There's one in the little children's farm up in the park. A male and yet his beauty is feminine, the pitch black of his eyelids like mascara, his pearshaped eyes under the long lashes almost erotic.

He reaches for the apple in the palm and lets the stranger pet the warm white and bristled fur of his huge head, his cavernous nostrils puffing plumes of warm air in the morning chill. The great ears twitch as the stranger whispers into them.

Dear donkey, dear green teeth and muddy fur, dear ammonia odor of steaming turds, dear little farm tucked away in a cancerous city, dear earth, let the stranger sleep with you tonight, he's longed for you all his life.

He stretches his neck across the velvet moss of an old weathered fence and an answer rises from deep in the trumpet of his bray, a little shrill at first as if it were struggling to squeeze through the channels of his neck and then finally vibrating full-throated and swollen like an echo from the underworld, a seed syllable from the buried light.

"*Haw*, he used to cry, *hee-haw*, *hee-haw*, as if he were talking to me. I haven't been near a donkey in seventy years and yet I still remember his face. Probably because I've seen pictures of donkeys. Pictures help to remember."

Boys and Girls

No photos of us that year in London but Dolores took a few of her darling son Luigi all bundled up in his stroller, his ersatz uncle taking him for walks in the Heath.

"*Andiamo alla selva!*"

"*Andiamo alla selva!*"

The snow heavy that winter and the Heath white for many weeks, a new and exciting country then and not yet Americanized, clean and simple as we strolled down the lanes and watched the English world go by, everywhere sparkling through his eyes and the air bursting with light as we rolled down the hills in the sunny frozen afternoon.

"*Ancora! Ancora!*"

His eyes clear and wide like windows into the lost world.

We carried him on our shoulders like donkeys under a savior. We undressed him and watched him as he sat on the toilet and then we wiped his shitty ass. We buttoned him and zippered him and tied his shoes as if he were a prince, the miniature Buddha all infants resemble.

We fed him bits of cheddar cheese and whole-wheat McVitty biscuits and the meat that was so expensive. Yet how little it takes to feed a child, a little food and love all the time, and then we would lie with him and lull him into sleep with a book of giant animals, his knee up and his arm out and the other curled with a thumb in his mouth, half Dolores and half Charlie and yet no more theirs than the light itself, the eternal child buried in each of us.

How could we but love each other when we see that child inside?

In ourselves on that motor scooter like it was the bike you got for Christmas when we were kids, your hair crazy in the wind and the eyes behind you, the hair you always worried about.

"You're lucky you don't have to worry about the future, you old bald bastard."

"Fuck you, Charlie."

All the way down Haverstock Hill to the West End, the young males on the hunt for experience, for the baguettes from the market by what was that street with all the wagons and then the stout in what was the name of the pub that later became so popular, Soho in those days still unpolluted and vital, Old Compton Street full of familiar faces and the cold wet air alive with politics, the pubs opening after the galleries closed and the guys from the Institute coming over to throw darts over a couple of pints, London the family town full of old polished brass and ancient wood, everywhere carpeted and old-fashioned and none of us with any money, every day rich with art and each other and all the books and films, films and more films at the new N.F.T. or the private room at the B.F.I. or the small sordid theatres from Clapham to Islington for half a crown or even less. How many times did we see *Seven Samurai*?

Meanwhile came the news from the States, the three young men killed in Mississippi and thrown in a ditch, the young people our age who went down there and put their lives on the line.

We studied Picasso while kids got bashed, we studied Joyce while some got murdered. Was art worth our struggle while others suffered, what good was composition against a cannon or a bomb?

Yet as other young men once hunted or fought so too would we be warriors with our eyes.

This we shared that made us brothers, the need to leave a mother's kitchen and strike out in search of what, where was the thunder and the light that would redeem our selfish hours?

Down Dean Street and through the Chinese Quarter we headed for the lions in the Square. *Comon, Zekey, let's hunt the lions, let's climb the mountain and find the treasure.*

Up, up we climbed the steps of the Gallery as if it were our cave, the cardboard forts we used to build on the sidewalk and wouldn't let the girls come in because they were girls. This was the boy's cave and only he could draw on the wall, the girls had to go find their own cardboard.

Yet what were the pictures and who were the bison who became the gods who turned into apples? They were all feminine and all forms were the body of a woman.

Beauty was a woman and the great delta every artist tried to fuck, the battlefield plowed and planted for one more time to see her blossom, all the heroes buried inside, blind Degas and deaf Goya and phobic Cezanne and poor Vermeer and poor Daumier and all the others poor and crippled, each one's picture glowing on the wall as she stared back through their different visions.

We stood before her like little boys, you standing by Piero's *Baptism* with your pants slipping from your waist because you never wore a belt, your narrow hips and small buttocks low in your squat muscular frame, your cuffs crumpled derelict around your old sneakers and a hole in the sleeve of that green sweater your friend's mother knitted and that you stole because you wanted it and then wore until it fell apart.

You also wanted her, a novel about water and light and a story about a boy's first communion, all those lines you kept revising.

You stood in front of the visionary glow and didn't move, a dove hovering over a golden cup, a young woman staring from behind a tree, your old sneakers and denims fusing as if in double exposure with the luminous figures of John pouring water over Jesus' head.

You were beautiful in your devotion to art, the *paisan* who would share the poverty and struggle that lay ahead. Together we would endure and survive in the jungle of the marketplace. With friendship and a common goal we would hold out against the isolation and rejection. Our love of art would keep us together. We would trade clothes and tools and we would help each other move from one rent to another. We would carry all those books and paintings from one city to another as if they were our seeds for a better farm. We wouldn't let hospital bills or jalopies defeat us. We would be artists and we would share our meals through the cold winters of enormous heat bills.

Christmas came and we stood in Smithfield's Market and bid for a turkey, the slaughter of that turkey becoming the feast we shared with Leo and Tony coming over from Paris with cognac and wine, the drunken happy night we sat around a paraffin heater and wrote a communal letter to Shlomo still back in New York, and in the early morning drunkenness we read the old-age poems of Yeats whom we loved so much.

No photos but the memories still vivid. They fuse now as if in double exposure with a night twenty years later at Joey Russo's funeral, the shock of your hair gone white and the sudden crack in our ten year silence, our words empty in the void of Joey's death. *Hello Zeke. Hello Charlie. How you doin? Fine, and yourself? Oh I'm doin okay.* Joey in the casket and death in your crow's feet, our words dying before they could express our love.

We loved each other and that winter night in London when it was your turn to stay home with Luigi your friend would have enjoyed going to the film with you as much as with Dolores.

She's not my wife, he wanted to tell the eyes on the bus, don't look at me as if I'm her husband, her husband is my friend Charlie.

But when she put her hand inside his arm it burned through his coat with the memory of you telling him how when you first kissed her you almost came in your pants.

"Aren't these busses nice, Zeke? I love to ride on the top of them."

She was so young, younger even than the women who now seem like girls. Dolores, called Didi by her brothers, the daughter of Mario and Ida, the former clarinet in a highschool marching band, a bump in her nose and a gap between her teeth, another beautiful young woman.

But she was not really Dolores. She was the girl who didn't know who she was and didn't trust anyone who thought they could. She was the girl who wanted to change her name and looked in the mirror as if it were a painting she could wipe away and start all over again.

The theatre was that small and cosy one in Hampstead and of all films it was the one by the young Truffaut, *Jules and Jim*, an old man's story of two friends and a woman in between.

The seats were tight and the touch of her knee was like a shock to the one who sat next to her and tried to avoid it and then wanted it again, wanting and avoiding as the sentimental music quivered up his spine and through his loins.

She was not really Dolores to him either. She was what's her name, that girl who wore pennies in her loafers and lived above Kowit's Department Store. She was the girl who lived who knew where on the other side of town and you were always making fun of a crazy Zeke who kept looking for her. She was all the bus-stops and ice-cream parlors and all the running and waiting for just a chance to say hello. She was that girl who appeared one morning when you were sick and two volunteers were needed to split your paper-route and there on Paterson Plank Road where the busses stop on their way to the suburbs she was standing with her schoolbag in another vision in the half light. "Yeh, I know who you mean," you said disdainfully the next day, "she's dat gurl who goes to a private school." "Whadda you doin here?" you would say on the following days. "Your route aint near here. No, I don't know where she is and I don't give a shit." She either moved or took another bus because she was never there again, the impossible one, the one in the distance, eventually your wife.

She was not really Dolores, she was our youth and the blind rutting passion only youth can know. She was the female we would have bashed our foreheads for were we not human, our horns locked for the rest of our lives while she wandered off with another male.

She was the young woman in the next seat who felt high when the

film was over. It was a contagious film in those days and she too was
infected by the hypnotic screen and the need for fantasy.

"Let's not take the bus back, Zeke. Let's walk instead."

Her heels clicked on the pavement like an instrument in the thick
fog.

"Oh, Zeke, isn't it a lovely night?"

And she took the hand of her partner and swung his arm as if in a
dance. No, he was the one who took her hand, but what difference
does it make, both of them were equally blind in the amber glow of
the fog and the ignorance of their youth. They didn't know themselves
or each other and they swung their arms as if holding the hands of
strangers, the fog so thick that all they could see were the sulfur
streetlamps glowing with that soft yellow light as if in a dream.

And, as if they were a kind of brother and sister in their blindness
and passion, she trusted him and wanted to tell him something but
didn't know what it really was.

It came out in a story about a boy in her childhood.

"His name was Richard. I always looked at him but when he looked
back I turned away."

She had her own vision, a boy who disappeared.

"I knew he liked me but then he moved and I never saw him again."

No, she was not Dolores or Charlie's wife, the angel in the kitchen
who never complained or the soft and gentle nurse who made great
lasagna and blushed when she farted. She was a little girl who had a
boy glowing inside her.

"Sometimes I dream of him even now. Sometimes I'm walking in
the street and I think I see him. Isn't it strange, I have this boy inside
me I don't even know?"

No, she was not a mother who rinsed shitty diapers in the toilet or a
quiet wife who let her husband do the talking. She was the girl who
never grew up, the lost child in search of herself.

"I went away last summer, Zeke. It was before you came. Charlie
stayed with Luigi and I went away."

She was still unformed when she became a mother, she who needed
one of her own.

"I hitchhiked to Dover and then I hitchhiked all the way to Italy."

She was Miss Everywoman who wanted to explore and who smiled
with selfishness and excitement when an old truckdriver picked her

up in Germany and treated her to sauerbrauten. She wrapped her arms around her breasts and snuggled into her dreams in a tiny room of a strange hotel.

"And no one knew where I was. There I was completely by myself and no one knew anything about me."

And outside her role of mother and wife she tried to paint her self-portrait with an image of freedom and adventure, her hair in the wind and her thumb behind her shoulder.

"And I wanted to keep going, Zeke. I wanted to go to Greece, I wanted to go to Turkey, I wanted to go to India, I just wanted to keep going, I didn't want to go back."

And her words were like a sudden smear in the ideal picture her audience had painted of her marriage. What did she mean, not go back?

"The thought of Luigi kept pulling me back and the further I went the more I thought of him. Yet something in me wanted to keep going, I didn't want to go back. There was something in me that could have left my own child."

She wasn't talking to her partner anymore. She was talking to the fog, the amber glow like a beacon back to her iron fence and her ivy-covered bricks. She was longing for something she couldn't find in her husband or her child. She was looking for it in the fog.

"Something in me was so selfish that I ignored my own child."

She went back to her home, but her words grew inside her confidant like whatever it is that causes an earthquake, something deep and always burning.

She had that same burning. We all had that same burning, and the years passed with it growing not only in our personal lives but everywhere else in our famous decade of naked girls in huge crowds and boys from Vietnam in plastic bags.

It flamed in psychedelic colors and mushroomed like whatever it was down deep that cracked the surface and ripped our lives asunder. The end of your marriage was like a crack that would sunder us apart who all gathered like a family in your home.

Almonds and The River

- In my village we ate almonds in the spring when the nut was like milk and the green shell still soft.
- I don't remember much about where I lived.
- I remember my hometown very well. I can even tell you the names of the streets.
- They don't have those names anymore.
- The Moslems live there now.
- They're supposed to be very poor.
- Let them be poor and more poor.
- Don't say that.
- Why not?
- They don't know what happened. They weren't even born then.
- So what?
- So have compassion.
- For a filthy Moslem who lives in my father's house?
- You don't want that house anyway.
- You got a better house here.
- I got two houses here, so what?
- So let them live there.
- They have no right to live there. Let my own people live there.
- Who?
- Not me.
- I'd go for a visit.
- What for?
- She misses her almonds.
- I have an almond tree in my backyard.
- Not for the almonds. For the river.
- What river?
- The river where I played when I was a child.
- Oh you and your river.

She Holds The Fort

My children are my life, says the mother, let them do what they want as long as they love me. And if one of them wants to draw cowboys on the wall, let him, I won't wash them away. Let him make a mess, let

him do anything he wants as long as he's not a corpse at the side of the road. Art? It is what he scribbles on the porcelain table while he waits for dinner. Let him make a life of it if he chooses, I'll wipe the table clean for him to scribble some more. Let him choose poverty and I'll send him a check, let him stay away for years and we'll talk on the telephone, let him anything, dear life, but don't let him disappear. For I am no one if not a mother. My elements are the skillet, the grinder, and the mortar and pestle. I am my knife and my bowl and my pot and my roller. I live by the Hoover, the Maytag, the General Electric and the Singer. I wear curtains and bedspreads and change them all the time. My home is my laundry and my hands are for work. Don't give up, my son, clean your studio if you get lonely, go shopping, cook soup. Look at me, I always find something to do.

And her voice becomes the song of survival, the music of food and warmth.

The grinder clamps with a wing nut on the old wooden chair and the loop of its arm squeaks the cold flesh into the spiral. In the butcher's window the lamb hung headless like a slaughtered baby, but now in her kitchen the chunks of a shoulder transform in a gyre and become food for her sons, the red coils writhing like the worms of life. Watch your finger as you feed the cup. Cousin Aram caught his finger in the hole when he was a kid and to this day his fingernail grows crooked.

Turn and turn to the rhythm of death into food. Course ground for the filling, the fine for patties. The first she fries with onion and allspice, the other she mixes with bulghur and shapes into delicate cells. Then she spoons in the filling and pats them into perfect cells with a crease at the edge. They are difficult to make because they must retain air when boiled so that the form will make a little *piff*! of steam when it pierces them. *Kuftah*! With a glass of yoghurt in ice water and some radishes and carrots.

She is her kitchen, the source of *zahd*, the warm meal. She is the Ma of stuffed eggplant and zucchini, of stuffed cabbage and grapeleaves and even lettuce and cucumber and gutskin and tripe. She is the Ma of multifarious stews created from lack of meat so that with only a few marrow bones and garlic come the spicy okra and fava beans and stringbeans and turnips, their juice to join the everpresent bowl of the overflowing heap of bulghur, our common seed. During the Depression old Nevart fed her seven kids with bulghur alone. The other kids in the street don't know what it is. They never even heard of it. They got their own food. All kinds of food and the different recipes created with a reverence for where they came from.

Food, fodder to bone, families enjoying the taste of kindred creatures, the dogs grinding the bones into polished wampum. The life-substance, the juice of death. Drink it to survive. Lemony spinach soup and big spiced balls of crushed garbanzo. *Potcha* of tripe with feet and skull, the eyeballs dissolving in the boiling marrow. *Shok-humtoolshi*, the fermented turnip and carrot drink cousin Khosrof calls Superman Water. Extravagant *paklava* and *boreg*, crisp *tabouli* and a potpouri of *guvaj*, green, crimson, ochre and mauve in the odor of the centuries. Her spice shelf a treasure of bark and seed from an ancient past, each one with a label she can't read. The coriander in the *Noxema* jar, the cumin in the little *Gerber* jar, the rolls of cinnamon in the *Johnson and Johnson* tin, the fennel seeds in an empty ink bottle. Crush them into powder in the old grinder with the worn wooden box. Open the little drawer and pour the magic from a history of a specie forever cooking. The recipe for *choreg* goes back three thousand years and the black sesame comes from land of Gilgamesh. When a baby's first tooth pierces the soft gum the seeds are crushed and mixed with sugar for celebration. Grind and pound them as ancestors once did while Xenophon marched by, or famished Crusaders, or screaming Mongols. From her warm kitchen come recipes for weddings or remedies for aches, *henna* to stain the pinky in the bride's house and olive oil in an onion slice for an ear infection, okra for boils and dough for bruises.

Her kitchen is a link in the cycles of *doon*, *domus* through the ages. Four stories high in a row of rooms facing at one end the Empire State Building across the river and at the other the blue western hills beyond the garbage dumps. Italians across the hall and Irish next door, some Swiss and Germans and a few Jews, the Cubans waiting for the next generation.

Doon she defends against the mice and the roaches and pleads with the landlord for hot water and heat. "Please, Mr. Russo, my wash no good wid no hot water." She churns the steamy foam with a short stick and lifts the heavy sheets from the loud chug-a-chug of the powerful blades. She feeds the wringer and it spews the flattened slabs into a rolling heap by the window. She leans beyond the sill into the changing weather of each Saturday morning and the steaming sheets billow in the winds from the corners of the world. Sit on the fire-escape and watch how neatly they issue like sails from her nimble fingers. And now come the bright flannels and towels to join the other families in the common backyards, all the different lives swaying from the wash-poles like sails and pennants of explorer ships, of the Nina and the Pinta and the Santa Maria, the little tomato gardens like a port of call.

And then one day the line breaks and has to be strung again. Up, up the iron spikes to the crow's nest so high above, higher and higher holding tight, the pulley like the mystery at the end of a beanstalk, the perilous mast swaying in the wind and she in the window smiling with fear and pride. "Good boy, my sweet son."

She holds the fort. She keeps the refrigerator full, she stays by the stove and the sink. Leave her there to reconnoitre in the wilderness outside her den. Go down to the *Avenue* and enter it through the vestibule of white tiles and brass mailboxes.

No bushes, no trees, but the street is like a forest of different shops with vegetables and dry goods on the sidewalk and the trolley clanging under the wires, the junkman's horse plopping turds on the cobbles and the vendor singing the names of fruit, a wild kingdom with different creatures in their habitats.

The old Chinaman with a mole by his nostril and a gold front tooth, his back bent to the ironing board and an oriental beauty on the calendar by the shirts, the odor of steam and incense and stinky pork fat wafting through his back door.

The tall scary Italian barber with the soft hands and the pencil stripe mustache and that terrible electric clipper hanging from the wire, his sheet tight around your neck as you sit on the hard board over the arms of the chair and a nude on a calendar with flowers between her legs, the odor of bay rum almost edible as he twirls his big brush in the mug and slaps his leather like a hit man.

The small chunky Italian shoemaker with black fingers and nails in his mouth, a loud opera on his scratchy radio and the inviting odor of glue and leather, the shoes on the counter like living things.

Mr. Pinsky, the Jewish grocer with his old marble counter always covered with tub butter and cream cheese and the strange red fish.

The shadow people in the dangerous saloon with the juke box and the dank odor of whiskey, the tiny red and blue lights glowing in a speluncar darkness and the figures immobile like ghosts, the tavern at the side and the huge steaming cartons of the exotic *Ah-beetz*.

The drugstore of colored bottles and the mysterious pharmacist always hidden in the rear.

The gibbous Jew in his tiny watch-repair shop and his eye always buried in his black cup.

The beauty parlor of that disgusting putrid odor and the women who sit in helmets like Frankensteins.

The realty office so foreboding and official with secretaries and men in suits.

The great Belli's delicattessen with the hanging cheeses and the moldy salami and Mr. Belli always waving his arm like an opera singer and his beautiful daughters helping him after school.

The rich Mr. Kowit's little department store with the quiet aisles and the clean wooden floors and the soft comforting odor of cloth.

The Swiss bakery of jelly doughnuts and bright florescent lights and the Italian bakery of Mr. Petrangelo powdered with flour.

The Bijou where each Saturday afternoon everyone rolled empty soda bottles under the seats and sucked Sugar Daddies to Abbott and Costello and The Durango Kid.

And finally and most important of all, Mr. Silverberg's Confectionary, or as it is really called, *The Candystore*, the only place where money really matters, its window full of chocolates and cigars.

All the other shops could disappear but this one is essential, it is the source of sweetness and comic books, it is the fountain of gratified desire.

But it costs money and Mr. Silverberg is always watching and not wanting anyone to hang around if he's not going to buy anything.

But stand anyway in the alcove of the comics, the chapel of Classics Illustrated and Captain Marvel and all the figures who will become the nudes and saints of future museums.

And if you have a nickel you can stand by the counter and make a big decision between strawberry, chocolate or vanilla, vanilla fudge coming soon.

This is what life is all about, colored pictures and sweet milk. But it costs a nickel, the great buffalo on one side and the Indian on the other.

And then one day, maybe because the factory work was good that week, she has a quarter in her hand. A whole quarter!

"For me?" "Yes, for you." "And I can buy anything I want?" "Yes, you can buy anything you want."

What? What is there to buy with more money than you know how to use? How much pleasure can you take?

Run, run to the Candystore and point to the most extravagant item, the impossible thing, the thing you never could afford, the overflowing sweetness that would never end, the *Giant Hershey Bar*.

Bring it back to her with pride like the cat with a dead bird.

But she does not smile and she seems disappointed.

"Is that what you bought?"

It was not the right choice. What would have been the right choice? How can you please her and win her love? Look, Ma, look what I did, look what I found. A silver ball from the foil of gum wrappers and cigarette packs, a raft of dried popsicle sticks to sail in the gutter puddles, a collection of bottlecaps for scully on the sidewalk, a treasure out of garbage, the jewels of the wild neighborhoods, the beginning of art.

Horsechestnuts in the park with the cannon and the names of the dead. Hoses and bolts in the huge carbarn where the buses sleep like giant animals. Spools and cardboard from the embroidery factory to build a fort on the sidewalk. A mop handle for a spear, a rubber band for a sling. "Comon, Charlie, let's go down by the burlesque where the gangsters live." By the monastery where the mysterious nuns do who knows what behind the gate. By the stadium where the big guys carry duffle bags. By the cliffs that drop to the railyard and the barges on the waterfront, the Nazis and Fascists hiding among the freight cars. "Zekey, watch out! Over there, over there!" "Run, Charlie, we have to get to the river or they'll kill us. We'll be safe by the river."

What lives across the river? What treasure is buried in the great castle of the skyscrapers on the other shore? The colorful tugboats pull the gravid Queen Mary upriver from the bay. The sun falls and the palisades rise like totems in the dusk. Someday you will cross it and not have to worry about getting home late.

"Zak-kay, do you know what time it is?"

Her worry is the price of her warmth, she doesn't let go.

"Come sit down to dinner."

But let her hold on for a while. The night is demonic and the monster can climb the fire-escape. She keeps it away with clean sheets and a bath on the weekends.

In the tub her great white body grows pink in the steam. Stand between her legs while she sits on the small wooden bench and pours hot water on your head. Yell at her when your eyes sting from the soap or when she rubs too hard with the flaxen glove. Just don't look between her legs.

Yet her flesh has no sex, it feels as familiar as food or clothing. On the couch in the parlor she sits in her burnoose towel and cuts her toenails like an animal at the end of a long day's labor.

Now all is well in the flannel softness of faded pajamas and the odor of detergent. The pattern of the rug in front of the radio is rich with *The Fat Man* and *The Life of Riley*. In the morning there will be honey on the *hatzov-dabag* and she will be home ironing. The hills beyond the marshes and the castles across the river will all have to wait until you're ready to leave.

Beautiful Bodies

· I remember Lucia's body in the bathhouse. She was so beautiful she felt ashamed.
· She didn't feel ashamed. The old women made her feel ashamed.
· What mouths they had.
· Now we have them.

· Do we? My granddaughter doesn't even wear a brassiere and do I say anything?
· When I was her age I couldn't even shave my legs without the old women calling me a whore.
· What happened to the bathhouse?
· I think it's a Cuban restaurant now.
· I remember the horse-stables in the back of it and the smell of horse-shit.
· How much fun we had there.
· Now men and women sit together. Everything showing, even between their legs.
· They just sit in a big tub.
· Do they make music?
· I don't know what they do.
· They smoke dope.
· Good, let them smoke dope.
· My son-in-law put one of those jacuzzis in his bathroom.
· Oh yeh? I want one too.
· I don't need any jacuzzi. I like a good *keesah* on my body.
· You can't get that flaxen cloth anymore.
· My granddaughter wants one. She likes old-fashioned stuff.
· She has a beautiful body, your granddaughter.
· I hope it's not too beautiful. Look what happened to Lucia.
· It's not easy to be beautiful.
· My mother had to smear herself with shit so they wouldn't rape her.
· My granddaughter doesn't have to do that.
· They learn to fight now. They do that Japanese stuff. I saw on the news a woman who broke a man's nose when he tried to rape her.
· Good for her.
· Did they catch him?
· Yes, they caught him in the hospital when he went for his nose.

Woman Bathing

"I remember my mother taking me to the bathhouse. I remember walking with her while she carried the sack with the towels and the *footahs*. The bathhouse was called *hamam* in Turkish and the women went on Fridays and the men on Saturday nights. I remember the big door that pulled open with the heavy iron ring and I remember the deep echo that boomed through the halls."

They enter the chamber of laughter and splashing, mother and daughter to a tiled stall.

They undress and wrap themselves in their *footahs* and they take their place by a bucket.

The water crashes through the halls and the wet sheets cling to shiny flesh, Moslem and Christian alike in the veil of steam.

Women bathing. Degas' woman bending over. Titian's woman twisting her hair. Rembrandt's woman lifting the hem of her gown above her knees. Rubens with her arm raised, Ingres' with her back turned, Renoir's with her hand between her thighs. Durer's, Cranach's, Cezanne's, Roualt's. Lovely or noble, wrinkled or nubile, desirable or pathetic through the ages.

She washes her breasts and cups them with her palm as if to milk the eyes of her passionate grandson.

He's obsessed with the crease of her buttocks and the swell of her nipples, the hair of her mound and the lips inside them.

He has wanted to see her naked ever since he was not supposed to, the darkness under her dress and the contour of her bodice like mysteries he has wanted to solve ever since the dream of seeing Miss Savio's cunt in the first grade, her legs open under the desk and the hem of her skirt over her knees.

She was the mysterious female always wearing clothes. She was an executive in a suit, a dancer in a leotard, a lovely hygenist with an elbow in the crotch of her uniform as she bent over to clean some teeth.

She was that woman in the Ganges who washed herself underneath her sari while the waves lapped her breasts and her hair glowed in the long spokes of a dying sun, her nimble fingers washing both her hair and the sun as if she were dancing, her head bending as she plunged the brilliant mass into the waves and then swung it around and curled it easily into a bun while a garland of marigolds floated downstream from where an arm of a corpse softly dropped into the ashes of a flaming pyre.

She was the secret underneath the clothes of the flesh, the darkness in the eye sockets of a cadaver on the sand, her stench drifting through the years.

She sits with her daughter in their burnoose towels and enjoys the pleasure of cleanliness and grapefruit. She peels the shiny globes into the ruby slivers of the juice, so delicious and refreshing and each dewy cell of the tartness like a teardrop.

The Salesman With The Eye Infection

· I was sitting in the garage the other day and a man came up to me.
· The garbage man.
· No, not the garbage man. I didn't know who he was and then he said, "May I speak to you for a minute?" "Why sure, I said, why not?" "Oh, thank you," he said. "None of the other women will even open their door."
· I don't blame them.
· I was just sitting there and he looked like a nice man.
· Of course he looked nice. He was probably a salesman.
· He was a salesman. "Madam," he said, "you don't have to buy anything. I just need to talk to three people a day for my job."

· They all say that.

· Let her finish.

· "Why sure," I said. I wasn't doing anything. I finished my work and I was just sitting there. So then he brought his machines from his car. "Oh no," I said, "I'm happy with my Hoover." "Please," he said, "I need to demonstrate it at least three times." So he came into my house and he vacuumed all the rooms. And when he finished vacuuming he started shampooing and I tell you he must have worked for an hour and when he was done my house was as clean as my dishes.

· What were you doing?

· I wasn't doing anything. I just sat there and watched him.

· Only in this country can a man come into your house while you sit and watch.

· And you didn't buy anything?

· Why should I buy anything? But I did tell him what a nice job he did. "Thank you so much," I said, "your cleaner is wonderful, but I'm happy with my Hoover. I'll give your card to my friends."

· Don't give it to me.

· He was a nice man. I wanted to give him something to eat but he even had his own lunch. "How about some coffee?" I said and he said okay, so we sat in my garage and he ate his lunch and we drank coffee.

· You got your whole house cleaned for a cup of coffee.

· He could have had more if he wanted. He sat and talked with me for almost an hour. He told me about his eye infection. He said he went to a doctor who didn't know what it was from and told him it was probably some kind of allergy.

· They all say that. Whenever they don't know what something is they call it an allergy.

· I told him he needed mother's milk. When I was a girl I had an eye infection and my mother took me to a young woman who was nursing her child and she put her nipple by my eye and let a few drops fall in and a few days later my eye was okay.

· I'm sure your salesman would like that whether his eye got better or not.

The Cotton and The Pig

"I remember cotton. When I first came to California I saw cotton in the fields and I told my friends to stop the car so I could get out and touch it. It was a windy day in autumn and all the cotton was spilling from the husks and flying in the wind. It took me back to my child-hood and I held it to my face. It made me remember my mother and the big tent where she went to work in the wintertime and the big mounds of cotton inside and all the women pulling it apart."

It bursts from the sidereal husk, the oily seed buried in the white-ness, the cousin to the hibiscus and the okra.

Her hands are raw from too much of it. The acre is enough for food but not for extras. There must be school for the boys and a dowry for her daughter. She keeps working, she is never still.

"I sewed cotton all my life and never connected the cloth to the big mounds in the tent where my mother worked. Fifty years I worked in the factory and I never thought of the cloth as the same white stuff that made me so happy when I saw it again in the fields."

How strong it feels in the form of canvas. Not as fine as linen but still dependable for a ground, the stretch as tight as a drum and the gesso seeping through the double weave, the white field for another figure, the avatar of ten cents an hour and an aching back.

She begins to emerge with the bristles of a pig, a number six filbert loaded with sienna. What face could redeem the slaughter of that pig and its life in a pen too small for it to move?

Shrimp Like Fingers

· We can go to Lake Tahoe for sixty dollars and they give us back thirty to spend. Araknaz went with the church group. The bus, the motel, the food, everything for thirty dollars.
· They want people to gamble. They know once people start they don't want to stop. There's nothing else to do there anyway.
· You said it. When I was in Las Vegas I stood at the machine all day.
· No, Araknaz kept the thirty dollars and walked around and then went to bed at eight o'clock. But she said she had a good time. She said she ate shrimp and they were as big as her finger.

· Let's go. Thirty dollars, it's nothing.

· What do you think, they throw money in the streets in this country.

· Whenever my son has pennies in his pocket he throws them in the
  street.

· They throw food in the streets.

· Araknaz didn't. She put what she couldn't finish in her napkin and
  brought it home and ate it for lunch the next day.

· I hope they have shrimp again. I like shrimp.

· My husband loved all fish. He was from Istanbul. He never ate meat,
  only fish. His own brother was a fisherman before he was slaughtered.

· I didn't know they slaughtered us in Istanbul too.

· He was in the underground.

· My uncle was in the underground too. I remember visiting him in the
  jail. I was the only one allowed because I was so young. "*Yavrim*," he
  said, "don't ever forget who you are. Promise me you will never forget who you are." And I had to promise him I would always remember who I am.

She Seemed Impenetrable

Dearest Zeke," Dolores wrote in one of her letters after Mimi was born, "I hate words when they are so dull and the joy I feel is so impossible to express. Everything about my pregnancy, delivery, and post-partum was beautiful and it was the most wonderful moment in our lives. I'm so sorry I was drugged when Luigi was born. Charlie was the sole reason for it going so well because he believed so firmly I could do it even when I was about to give up. But I loved him very much and it was impossible for me to do anything but go on. We watched together as Mimi's head came through and out and then as the rest of her seemed to explode from within me. I held her, blue, slimy, wriggling and screaming while the doctor cut the cord and I became ecstatic over the smell of the vernix which covered her body. I could not get enough of that fragrance and I buried my head in her neck and arms all the way to the nursery. I hated her to be washed."

She was the homeliest baby there and looked, as the cleaning lady said, 'like a tough guy.' She does in fact strongly resemble Charlie's grandfather. Charlie is mostly amused by her dead-pan expressions and her funny face and really hasn't spent much time with her. I think he is content to have felt Luigi's infanthood so strongly and will wait for Mimi to grow up a bit. Luigi loves her to tears. He is constantly hugging and kissing her and suffers terribly when she cries. He grows a bit impatient because she doesn't respond when he talks to her but she is his first concern when he awakens.

"We miss you very much and look forward to seeing you back in the States. You will love this old farmhouse we rented in the pineflats."

It was a wonderful place and she loved living there among all the rabbits and blueberries, little Mimi in her arm twirling tiny fingers in the tranquil rhythm of sucking, mother and daughter quietly gratified on a musty old mohair couch.

How impenetrable they seemed, the closed circle the eye could not fuck, her moist areola repellent to lust.

Then the schoolbus would crush gravel at the stop in the road and Luigi would jump down and run home. He would kick the door open and run to the couch for her other arm and to tell her what he did in school. You would not be back until dark and by then she would be buried in dishes and the gang coming out for a visit, the night filled with ashtrays and all the men talking about art. And yet for a short while in the afternoon there was only the calm chirping of sparrows like an accompaniment to Luigi spelling simple words.

You came home from work and sometimes you were okay and sometimes not. You were going to be thirty years old and your novel wasn't finished and maybe it never would be. You turned to her for something but she didn't have whatever it was that would fill the emptiness growing deeper inside you.

You plunged into chores and furniture as if they would save you, your home replacing your novel and becoming an art of two by fours and saw-horses.

You loved the wet and almost sweet odor of lumber and the soft touch of sawdust and maybe they would help you. You loved your hammer and the sensuality of a perfect fit and you loved to build and polish and to stand back and look. You loved the afternoons in the lumberyard and the pleasure of new words with the old men of the trade, the smooth delicious measure of stud and joist and the new language you could speak with those who didn't know Dostoievski from a hole in the wall.

You were Charlie again who could fix old cars and wasn't afraid of mechanics. You didn't need your novel published or your picture in a magazine. You were Charlie the fullback whom the whole team depended on. You held your daughter in your protective arms and taught your son how to fish. You were building a home, you were a man or so you tried to tell yourself.

You found a potbelly stove in the junkyard and some cheap wood to chainsaw for the winter. You were always good at finding things cheap, old furniture and rare books and old toys from the Thirties. You loved to collect things and fill your castle with them and show them to your pals as if they were the ballast of your journey through life.

But they were not enough and you were not enough and you turned to her as if she could provide what was missing.

No, she didn't have it, and you stayed up late and fed the fire with more logs, the flames flinging shadows from your big shoulders, your weight forward like an old buffalo with a hump on his back.

You kept drinking and the more you drank the more you wanted to arm wrestle and prove how strong you were. You stared into the flames with an empty bottle in your hand.

"Sometimes I look at her, Zeke, and I don't know who she is."

History

· My grandson's girlfriend came the other day to write recipes. She wants to cook for him, but she's an *odar*. I told her, "You have to live with me and cook with me to learn these foods."

· What kind of *odar* is she?

· I don't know, she says she's American.

· They all say that.

- I asked her what kind of American and she said a little of this and a little of that as if she were a recipe.
- There are no Americans. They just say that to make themselves feel like they're somebody.
- They're won't be anymore of us either.
- Not if we marry a part of this and a part of that.
- We will be gone when we lose the language.
- Why should anyone want to keep the language
- The language is everything.
- It gives us history.
- I don't like history.
- Let us be part of this and part of that.
- It's safer.
- What are you saying? Did my father die for nothing?
- I don't know why your father died.
- He died because he would not become a Moslem.
- So they ripped his nails out and slit him open with a butcher knife, that's better than being a Moslem?
- They would have done that even if he did become a Moslem.
- They ripped my baby daughter from my arms and threw her in the river. Do you think I could ever be a Moslem after that?
- They did something else to me.
- Christians do those things too.
- I'm not Moslem and I'm not Christian.
- What are you then?
- I'm a grandmother, that's what I am.

She Is Special and Unique

"What were the color of her eyes?"

"Do you think I could remember the color of her eyes and forget her face?"

"What about the color of her hair?"

"I don't remember her hair. I just remember her kerchief."

"What kind of kerchief?"

"What kind of kerchief? The kind all women wear. A kerchief is a kerchief."

They wear them in the news from El Salvador and Cambodia. She may have moved there or maybe to South Africa or the Philippines.

"What do you remember?"

"I remember only places and moments."

Olives curing in a dripping bag and the twang of a *sas*.

"My father played the *sas* and my mother used to sing. I remember some of the words but I can't remember her voice."

It flows through the years on eternal radio waves, someone somewhere clapping in rhythm to the dance of life, Moslem or Christian or

extra-terrestial. She taps the floor with her heel and sways her head to the music.

"We were poor but not as poor as those who swept the latrines and carried the shit away. We had our own acre and we had a lot to be thankful for."

She stuffs a sprouted seed in a furrow and lets the light provide, her landscape is far from a desert. And yet the night is cold with a fear no blanket can warm and she begins to whisper.

"I remember everyone being afraid. My mother was pregnant and my brother Arshag was probably sprouting hair above his lip. I remember my mother talking about her brothers who were killed in the last massacre. I remember her saying their throats were cut and they were left for the birds."

Yet she sang the same songs as the one who climbed the minaret and sang his praise to the same light: *Allah akbar. La ilah ila 'llah*.

"I remember my father saying we had to leave. He had cousins in Aleppo and we would be safe in Aleppo."

She is a woman like any other and yet she is not. She is different, she is special and unique.

She is Christian and her face is painted with the blood of crusades and the ink of a bible she couldn't even read.

It is the face of history, of a broken temple and an oven.

It is the face of an old black woman in Harlem who used to spit tobacco juice in a coffee can and call her young welfare worker her child.

It is the face of an Oglala Sioux in a general store at Wounded Knee.

All the faces of a personal and collective history that tells us we're different from each other, the face of the dog who is tortured in the name of yet another religion called science that tells us we are special and unique.

She is special and unique and therefore she will die.

"We left right away. We packed our things and left."

"Did you take the donkey with you?"

"No, we took the train. I guess we left the donkey behind."

The morning is crisp and clear and the rainclouds billow like cotton above the hills. Silent in the corral the donkey keeps to himself like a pariah among the horses. They neigh and bite if he comes too near. He is not horse enough to be with them who are more powerful and fast.

He lowers his head and his huge lips nibble the rock of sugar in her palm. She hugs and kisses him, the power animal who will become her consort in the realm of the dead.

Turkish Coffee And The Airport

· Read the mud in my coffee cup and tell my fortune.

· Old Oghidah should be here, she read good fortunes.

· That's because she was the best gossip-monger around. She used to go around smelling everyone's dirty laundry and then when she read your fortune she would know everything about you.

· But she always read a good fortune. Whenever she would read my coffee cup she would say, "See this cloud in the corner, my girl?" That's good luck coming." Then one day I said, "*Deegin* Oghidah, how can I believe you when you say everything is good luck?" "*Yavrim*, she said, "if you don't believe me, who are you going to believe?"

· After what she went through everything else had to be good luck.

· She loved coffee. She loved to roll her own cigarettes and drink coffee with everyone.

· With cardamon seeds. It was good luck if it had cardamon seeds.

· So what about my cup now?

· See this cloud in it. That's good luck coming.

· I don't care about any clouds. Just tell me if I'm going to Hawaii. I want to go to Hawaii on one of those love boats.

· I don't see a boat but I see an airport.

· Of course you see an airport. That's because you know I go there for lunch.

· You go for lunch at the airport?

· Why sure, I like to believe I'm going somewhere. You want to come?

The Foam Around Her Ankles

Art is the history of our youth, Coltrane's *My Favorite Things* on an old Atlantic Album and Shlomo's big lips when he whistled in tune, an old tattered copy of *Anabasis* and Leo's husky voice quoting in French.

"*L'eternite qui bâille sur les sables.*" Eternity yawning on the sands.

Write it, Charlie, you were the writer, write the song of our youth and the bright thalo colors of LSD, the bongos on the sidewalk and the dancing women who wore no bras.

And yet with all the sweetness of the Sixties, the fruit of the seeds planted in the beatnik pads of our underground Fifties, came the ghetto riots and the shock of the Tet Offensive, the photos and films for a history of bones.

We were not boys anymore and the dead were those kids too small to play with us big guys in the schoolyard, the poor jerks in the straight world with their cordovans and button-downs, their familiar faces staring back in the obituary of a centerfold in *Life*.

Write of how alive we were while kids kept dying, our wild love of art and the gloom of its impotence.

Write of our island and the great skyscrapers rising like familiar ziggurats in the middle of our biographies, our cab and postal routes and our caseloads of welfare and probation, our jobs on the dock or in the bank or wherever we could make a buck and go back to our canvases and our typewriters.

Write of our city of art and the child with her face blown off by mortar shell, Coltrane dying of booze and drugs.

Art is the only true history, the memory of a war in a magical rift, a plastic covered corpse in the song of the conqueror.

You were back in the city again, your farmhouse a heap of rubble.

"The landlord sold it to a developer. Dolores and I went out to take a look and we got there just as the bulldozer was warming up. Did you ever see a home get bulldozed, Zeke? It takes about ten minutes."

The plaster of our lives was beginning to crack, the bricks falling apart. You found a job uptown and Luigi was in the apartment with nothing to do and Uncle Zeke offered to take him to the beach.

"*Andiamo alla* beach!"

"*Andiamo alla* beach!"

We dumped the blankets in the old bug and pulled the sunroof back.

"Don't stand through there, Luigi, it's dangerous."

Yet fun and he kept poking his head through as we turned down Varick Street and made for the West Side Highway, only a few minutes to Brooklyn and the old reliable puttering under the new Verranzo Bridge, the great pylons silver in the hot clear blue and shiny afternoon, Dolores looking up.

"I love this bridge, Zeke."

There was a place to park near a retirement home and in the late afternoon during the week the beach was empty and the sand softly scalloped by the rivulets of shadow.

She laid Mimi on the blanket and then unbuttoned her blouse. She wore a modest brown and orange bathing suit and it was in one piece in order to hide her stretch marks. She lowered her skirt and stepped out of it, her thighs naked and a few pubic hairs escaping from her bold mound.

"What are you staring at, Zeke?"

"Nothing, I just never saw you in a bathing suit before."

"Really?"

"No, we were never together in the summer."

"That's true, isn't it? Isn't it strange after all these years?"

"Mama! Luigi yelled. Mama!"

She pushed herself up and led Mimi to the water and reaching with her other hand she pulled the seat of her bathing suit over the line of her buttocks as if to cover them from the one who walked behind her.

There was something about her that was different. She wasn't a sister anymore and the familiar years seemed to vanish like the foam around her ankles.

She bent over and gently splashed her ecstatic daughter who was screaming for more and yet more again. Then Luigi wanted her too and grabbed her thigh and tried to pull her in.

She hopped into the waves and her breasts and buttocks bobbed in the golden foam that rolled like a carpet from the low sun. Luigi jumped and dived and jumped again and the waves thundered and reverberated with a long hiss of bubbles that nibbled up the sand like fingers. When she came out her breasts heaved and her wet body flashed in a blaze of light. The waves rolled and hissed and then thundered

again as if to detonate the jetty of all honor and friendship. A man wanted his friend's wife. He wanted her so powerfully that he would have given up his friend in order to have her.

Have who, who was she he wanted with every fiber of the craving that sewed his winding sheet, the gulls hovering in the twilight of another sundown?

Rags

- Hripsimah is going. She's not the same Hripsimah.
- Sometimes she's the same and then she slips away.
- Well, she made it this far.
- Maybe she'll make it to ninety.
- She's already ninety.
- Well then ninety-five.
- Ninety's far enough.
- It's too far if I can't go to the toilet by myself.
- She's strong. She'll make it to ninety-five.
- She wants to see her granddaughter get married.
- Her children keep her alive. She lives for them.
- Didn't she have two others?
- She had two who died in the desert. She said she wanted to die then but she didn't.
- And now she wants to live.
- It depends on how she feels.
- I know that feeling. Sometimes I wake up and I want to live and sometimes I want to go back to sleep.
- If I don't work I get sleepy. I start to eat and then I get sleepy.
- What are you working on now?
- Rags.
- Rags?
- Yes, rags. Can you imagine that? My granddaughter wants a quilt made out of a patchwork of rags. It took me all my life to get out of rags and now my granddaughter wants to sleep in them.

Bricks

You found a job in New Hampshire for a month but she couldn't go with you. You didn't want to leave her but the woods would do you good and you'd come back all bronze from the outdoors and she'd love you like you wanted. Your voice through the phone was full of hope.

"Hey, Zeke, I leave tomorrow. Bring some of your mother's *dolmah* for my trip."

You kissed her long and deep and then you stepped into your partner's car.

"Take care of my family, Zeke."

You waved and the back of the old Pontiac became your back as you disappeared in the traffic. It was a pleasant morning and the heat had already started. She had to go to work that night and needed a baby-sitter.

Luigi liked fried potatoes.

"Here, Luigi, you can put the slices in. We let the oil get hot first and after we put them in they can't be moved."

"No, they don't like to be moved."

Mimi babbled in agreement, her walking and talking about to burst any day.

They nibbled the dead flesh and stems in innocence of any slaughter or famine.

"Tell us a story, Zeke. A story with a monster."

"You like monsters, don't you?"

"I love monsters."

After dinner Mimi lay on the bed with her legs up and her fingers twirling in her hole, her inscrutable eyes staring back at the familiar face who slobbered buzzing kisses on her navel and rubbed her anus and thighs with the cool cream. But when he came to her slit he paused as if it were forbidden, the delphic mystery of her coral lips clean and smooth like the washed marble of a ruin.

She lay in the darkness like a sibyl, her eyes open and the rubber nipple in her mouth.

In the living room Luigi was waiting for Huckleberry Finn. The clean sweet odor of his still chubby youth was almost heroic, his silken and feminine hair blending into the voices of the river and the lost world.

"Could we build a raft, Zeke?"

"Sure, we could do anything."

Explore the river and the beaver's castle, the hidden cave and the golden cup, the hills beyond the marshes.

"Where is Missouri, Zeke? Is it near New Jersey?"

After a chapter his eyes closed but he wanted one more. He was gone before the first page, his breath deep in the other world.

With both of them in bed the living room filled with the pleasant city sounds of the waning traffic and the muted jazz from the local bar. The red and blue paisley of the lampshade softened the light and the room seemed to glow like a hearth. The table glowed with the days you sanded it and oiled it and held hands around it saying grace. Dolores' curtains glowed with the night she cut and basted them. Luigi's toys glowed with their primal and totemic colors and the fern and the geraniums and the old throw rug all glowed with the image of *home*, the hut, the cave, the sacred fire, *domus* through the ages for the preservation of the specie and the need for roots, separate families with their own gods and photographs.

The bare brick wall was almost finished and just needed to be wire-brushed. You had wanted to expose the bricks because they reminded you of the old farmhouse, the soft sienna like the color of love and family. It had taken us all day to hammer the plaster off and carry it downstairs. We were happy together then, two old friends driving to the dump with their load of garbage, your face like a brother's while you bullshitted behind the steering wheel.

The gulls cawed over the steaming mounds, gulls and more gulls, an apocalypse of gulls, the giant wheels of a dinosaur tractor driving the refuse of our lives into oblivion, both of us staring into the pit as if it were the ruins of an ancient city rubbed away by a volcano, all those bricks and no one inside them.

Luck

· I said goodbye to Maritsa just in time.

· Was she awake?

· She was awake. I sat with her and when I left I said, "Maritsa, I'm going to say goodbye now." She looked at me and knew what I meant. "Goodbye," she said, "thank you for coming." I left and that night her son called me and said she died.

· She died good. She died in her own house.

· She was very lucky. I said to my granddaughter, "If someday you come to my house and find me dead, don't be sad, be happy, be happy that your grandmother died in her own house."

· They don't like to hear talk like that.

· They call the hospital and you know what the hospital does.

· They tortured Tarkoohi for two weeks before she was able to die.

· I hope they don't get me. I pray all the time that I can die before the hospital gets me.

· The hospital didn't get Maritsa but they brought a hospital bed to her house and she had a nurse to sit with her.

· She was very lucky.

· After what she was through in the desert she deserved some luck.

Hadeh Yalah

"I remember we took our bags and we went to the train station to get the train to Aleppo. We took our blankets and our pots, we had nothing else."

Last time they slaughtered her brothers like sheep, but she is not a sheep. Feel these hands and these arms, they are Grandma's hands and arms. They are roots of a life that grips hard and refuses to let go. They twist and resist and if they are severed they want to grow somewhere else. Someone tries to poison them or burn them but even then they may appear in another place. Feel how strong they are, these hands that smear and rub this virgin canvas.

She pulls the scallions she was growing in the boxes on the roof and after washing them in the bucket wraps them in the sheets of bread she baked last night. She wraps the curd cheese with more bread and ties it with the rest of the food in the calico rag, the pumpkin seeds and the dried chic peas and of course all the raisins, lunch and dinner for the long journey ahead and the water in a big green bottle with a cork.

Her husband wraps the seeds in other rags, the grape seeds and the squash seeds and the tomato and okra and bean and eggplant. Their new acre will be in another country and so too the baby that kicks inside her belly.

She sits in the station with her bags among the others in the motley of bedrolls and burlap on the platform. Her face is covered by a scarf and her husband stands quiet and worried.

Arshag is restless and teases his little sister. She yells at him and aware of her tension he doesn't answer back. He holds his paper and his pencil.

The station is dark and the gendarmes carry swords and guns. She sits on a wooden box and holds her belly. The train has arrived.

Everyone rushes for a seat and her husband holds one free for her by the window. She settles in and suddenly some Moslem friends from the acre come running up the platform to say goodbye. They are sorry they're late. They hold her hand through the window and wish her luck. She reminds them to get the donkey and care for it.

The train rolls and jerks and then starts moving, the landscape flowing across the window, the new green dappled with poppies and lupine. They would be tying the vines this time of year.

She keeps her face covered in the sooty roar of the coal dust and the loud mesmeric rhythm of the wheels. Her youngest boy, usually so naughty, sits quietly by her side, her daughter on her husband's lap and Arshag staring out the glass by the door.

She starts knitting.

"I remember the train stopping and the soldiers waiting outside with rifles and bayonets. '*Hadeh yalah*! they yelled. '*Hadeh yalah*!' And they pointed their bayonets and yelled, 'Leave the blankets and bags, you scum, leave them! Then they herded us onto the road that ran along a field of poppies and those purple flowers. '*Hadeh yalah*!' they yelled, '*hadeh yalah, hadeh yalah, hadeh yalah*!'"

Big Noses and Chechens

· Askig has a cousin who grew up in China. She speaks Chinese with her children.
· I heard there are some of us who made it to the end of Argentina.
· Where is Argentina?
· It's at the end of the world somewhere.
· Did they keep their names? Some of us don't keep our names.
· My name isn't my name anyway. It comes from a Moslem word.
· As long as it has our ending it's okay. Everyone knows who we are by the *ian*.
· Some of us in this town didn't want the *ian*. They took the *ian* off or even changed their names.

· How come?

· We were like dogs in this town while you and I were living back east. The signs here used to say, "No dogs or Armenians."

· Now we are the ones who own the signs and they say, "No Blacks and no Mexicans."

· They do?

· Why sure, you think we're any different?

· The Blacks and the Mexicans will own the signs someday and I wonder what they'll say then.
· Some of us could pass for Blacks or Mexicans. Jack-knife Nishan had hair so kinky he could pass for a Black in the summertime.
· The way you eat hot peppers you could pass for a Mexican.
· What about Indians? We used to play Indians in the movies.
· That's because of our big noses.
· I wonder how we got these noses.
· Once there's a big nose in a family it never goes away.
· Maybe the Indians got their noses in the same place.
· The Chechens were like Indians.
· You lived with the Chechens, didn't you?
· I lived with them for three years. After my family was slaughtered they took me for a slave. I spoke Chechen, I ate Chechen, and I would have had a Chechen child now if I hadn't escaped.
· How did you escape?
· I didn't really escape. There were merchants that passed over our plateau and I would give them notes to take with them. I would write my name and where I was.
· I did that too.
· I would have done that but I couldn't write.
· I learned how to write just in time. I had already been in school when that Chechen grabbed me and took me away on his horse.
· So did anyone find your notes?
· You know who found one of my notes? You know old Harry, the iceman?
· Why sure, he used to come to my home all the time with his pick in the ice and the burlap dripping on his shoulder.
· Well he found my note and he came to get me. But he had no money when he came and they would not give me to him so he had to go back and I had to wait another six months before he had enough to buy me from them. I think he gave them about ten dollars.
· Can you speak Chechen now?
· Not a word. Sometimes in my dreams I speak Chechen but when I wake I can't remember a word.

The Veil

When she returned from work the babysitter set the table as if she were his daughter coming home from a hard day at the playground. The red and green salad glistened under the lamp and the crusty bread from the bakery around the corner was still fresh and dusted with flour. He made her an omelette with mushrooms and peppers and poured her a glass of wine.

"Sit down and eat."

She slipped the shreds of lettuce in her mouth and chewed it slowly with her lips closed. Had she changed into her frock or did she still have her uniform on? Was her hair down or was it still in a bun? What comes most clear are the shadows from the lamp above the table and the reddish glow of the bricks, the vague and peaceful lull of the city sounds and the soothing waft of the humid breeze, the dark print of Rembrandt's little girl with a broom and the mesmerizing guitar of the Vivaldi concerto, the quiet and blurry colors like a tranquil foreground to a holocaust.

They would have a pleasant dinner and he would walk home by himself. They would slip into their roles of brother and sister and all his passion would have to go into his lines. They were alone together for the first time since the film in London and the glowing fog was now the sultry blur of a midsummer night. She began to talk as if she were continuing from where she had left off.

And yet her words came out of her mouth as if they were not her own but from a script on his forehead. She began asking him questions as if he were creating the scene that was beginning to unfold. She asked him about the women in his past and about Nelly.

"Did you love her?"

"Why do you want to know?"

"I don't know, I just asked."

She did something like chip the crust of bread with her thumbnail and slip it on her tongue and then nibble it sensually as if it were a sweet, the night itself almost succulent and the air lush and tropical, the pulse of the waning traffic like the slow and massive waves of a quiet sea.

Never before was she so intensely beautiful and not only her but the night itself and the kind of passion that always comes with ignorance, neither of them knowing the other and wanting something their illusions seemed to offer.

They paused and the throb of the silence was like a Judas sheep who led a herd to slaughter, all the years seeming to head for this moment like a line of sheep toward their destiny. The words came out of his mouth like an electric prod.

"You're the one I always wanted, Dolores, you were always the one."

Somewhere the wall seemed to crack but they both ignored it. It had started, the little crack they would never be able to stop, or rather it was there even before the bricks were baked.

Suddenly the quiet seemed ominous and they seemed to be on a bare and quiet stage like two actors shifting and looking for their places. She did something like center the bowl of flowers on the table and he walked around the room and came back. An audience seemed to shift in the corners of the room and if they looked they could see the children and the gang and the janitor and anyone else all hiding and pretending not to see as if to give them the illusion that they were alone and could do anything they wanted.

Would he? Would he step forward and press the little button that would blow the world away?

But maybe there was a better world and everyone would understand. He stepped forward and touched her hand and she held his fingers in a touch of yes.

No, cried the audience and the table and the curtains and the Vivaldi guitar and Rembrandt's little girl, no, take it back, don't do it, you don't know what you're doing.

But they knew they didn't know and in their recklessness they were both really the brother and sister they had played at for seven years and they both reached inside the other as if into themselves.

There seemed a sudden flash and after the pause the room seemed to tremble with the passionate thunder. It was done, there was no turning back.

Dear Charlie, he wanted to whisper, let me have my turn, let me know what it's like just for a moment, don't deny me this night.

But she was more lovely than he had imagined and he was not satisfied with just a night or a moment. He held on as long as she would let him and he could not get enough of her. He had finally found her, the one inside the pulse of the glow that would become an endless night.

She went to bed before the kids would get up and he stayed in the living room and watched the dawn through the veil of the haze in which nothing was clear but the heat and the throbbing.

Raisins

· You know how much lettuce costs?
· I don't care.
· Ninety-five cents a bunch. Ninety-five cents a bunch for lettuce.
· So what, you can afford it.
· I can afford anything but I won't buy lettuce. Me spend ninety-five cents for lettuce? I bought cabbage instead.
· I need to buy some cabbage. Our friend, the raisin man, wants me to make some *toolshee* for him.
· He needs more than *toolshee*. He must have lost a lot when the rains came too early.
· You think lettuce is high. Wait and see how much raisins will cost.
· I don't care, I got plenty from last year.
· I always keep raisins in the house. They keep me alive. Ever since the desert I keep raisins in the house. In the desert all we had to eat was a handful of raisins a day. Without those raisins I wouldn't be alive now.

She Dies

"It is all a dream to me now. I remember it like a dream. I remember she gave birth on the road and my father and I went to get some water for her. We walked very far and we came to a trickle in the some rocks and we filled the jars with the tiny drops.

At first there were oxcarts for the frail and the infant and some even had donkeys, but the Moslems grabbed them quick. Better to walk than fight like that woman who held on to the halter of her donkey on which her child was tied, the Moslem taking the child with the donkey and chopping her hand off with his scimitar when she tried to stop him.

"I remember some women with rings in their nostrils and black lines on their cheeks. I can't remember my mother's face and yet I remember those women with rings in their nostrils and black lines on their cheeks when we stopped and tried to find some water. You can find out who they were. You can read the books and learn who those women were and where they lived. You can read more than I can remember. You can read how far we walked. We went as far as Dar,ā. Can you find Dar,ā on the map?"

The line squirms between the cities like a caravan of death through the womb of history, the exotic names stippled in the cradle of civilization, each syllable a ditch, each letter a mound of skeletons, each city a prayer bead:

Ninevah whose breasts were sliced when she tried to rebel.

Palmyra who leapt in the river to escape but she could not swim.

Haran who leapt in the river because she could not swim.

Carchemish whose baby was ripped from her arms and flung into the river.

Gurgum whose baby's skull was crushed with a rock.

Tyre who dropped her baby into a well.

Tirqa who jumped into the well herself.

Damascus who came back from the well because it was full and hanged herself instead.

Antioch who was clubbed to death.

Ugarit who was ripped to death.

Sidon who starved to death.

Mari who smeared her hair with shit but he raped and killed her just the same.

Asshur who when her last child was slaughtered and someone tried to offer her comfort turned and said, *"Don't you see, don't you understand, God has gone mad, He wants to drink our blood."*

"My mother's baby was a boy and he was chubby and healthy but about a month later he died. I remember her telling me that he was sleeping and that I shouldn't go near him. My father buried him near Damascus and my father died in Damascus soon after. My younger brother died further on. I guess they caught some kind of disease."

They are naked but they are not nudes. The eyes gape, the arms flop out, and if a baby still clings to a breast the death was recent.

Nor are the hills a landscape, each wrinkle in the map a valley of screams and those who do not die keep walking through them. Limping. Prodded by the bayonet and whipped from the river and the shade. Attacked and raped by the brutal villagers who swoop from the hills with hatchets and clubs.

At one place the Moslem women themselves attacked with knives because to kill a Christian was to gain a home in paradise.

But they could not kill everyone and the rest kept walking. Eating weeds and grass and defecating where they slept. And with a few coins they swallowed to hide and then picked from their feces they bought water and life from the hoary merchant. *Give me gold or I'll kill you. Maybe I'll kill you just the same.*

"After my father and brothers died my mother and Arshag and I were going to escape to Jerusalem. I remember this clearly because I got a bug or something in my ear and I was very sick and we could not go on. That bug or something must have been my good fortune because I remember Arshag saying that all those who tried to go to Jerusalem were caught and killed."

A landscape by a master is an image of Eden and toward its vanishing point a caravan of culture skirts a river in a valley. That valley was once a kingdom and that river a route of art and song.

She rests with her son and daughter somewhere near an ancient city and a buried ziggurat.

In the vault of night the myriad stars are the same as above her acre. For every star a life and the void between them explains her hell, her body pocked with sores and her hair matted like the fur of a donkey, the strength gone from her hands. Her children curl asleep on the pebbles and she curls beside them. Another wail of pain and madness screeches from the other side of the camp.

Look down at her now as if from a satellite, her tiny body in a fetal curl, a vision floating above her like a hovering soul in the moonshine. She dreams of wheat and grapes and fresh milk and honey.

"One morning a soldier came and told my mother he would feed me and then bring me back at night. I don't know if she believed him or not but how could she say no?"

She had three sons and one daughter and disciplined her more because she was most like herself, wild and stubborn. She gives her to the soldier with all her faith in life. Don't die, dear daughter, stay alive, live, always live.

"She told me to go with him. '*Dudi*!' I cried, 'Mama!' 'Go,' she said, 'he will give you something to eat.' '*Dudi*!' I kept crying, '*Dudi*! *Dudi*! *Dudi*!'"

Mama, Mama, Mama, like the slashes of a palette knife.

Mama, Mama, Mama, the cry through the ages, mother and child ripped apart by the lord of the underworld.

"'*Hadeh yalah*,' the soldier said, and he took me away screaming. He took me to a train with the other children and they shoved us in a car like animals and I never saw her again."

She stays behind with her son. He is almost old enough to be taken as a young man and killed. But the smooth hairs above his lips are still like a woman's and he can still pass for a woman. She must find a dress for him, they must try to escape.

Dudi, he says, there is no escape. Don't say that, my son, don't lose hope.

Her daughter does not return and they keep walking.

Across the landscape and across the bodies, across the maps and the photos and the volumes of history.

And maybe she doesn't die. Maybe somewhere somehow they come upon villagers who let them stay and empty shit holes or sweep latrines instead of dying. Maybe they live in that village and sleep on rags and probe the garbage for food.

Maybe one day Arshag is scratching a picture of a sheep on a rock with a pointed stone and a master artist happens to be passing through that village and notices the picture and takes him on as an apprentice. Maybe Arshag earns enough to feed them both and they survive.

Maybe they live on another acre again. Maybe they make it to Yerevan or Alexandria or Argentina or Shanghai. Maybe Uncle Arshag has children in Shangai and they speak Chinese. Maybe they have a photo of her as an old woman in a straw hat.

Or maybe she is the old beggar who opened her palm in a ghetto of Benares. Maybe it was her bony fingers that scratched the window of that train? Maybe she is still there whispering *backshish*.

Backshish, backshish, backshish.

She lies buried in a valley, her bones the rocks now clean and smooth, her flesh the food for the meadow and the wood. Her eyes are the lupine and her voice purls in the breeze, her blood colors the petals of the rose.

She with her son in her arms like the Rondanini Pìetà.

She with her arms out like Piero's giant madonna.

She in Vermeer's girl with a turban.

She in Gauguin's Tahitian with mangoes in her arm and her breasts naked.

She in Rembrandt's Hendrickje with the hem of her gown above her thighs and she in all of Degas' bathers.

She stands in the photograph from the famine in Cambodia, a dead child in her arms and the bowl of rice at the end of the line too late to save him.

She is about thirty years old when she dies.

Killing and Sex

· They shot another diplomat.
· Who?
· Those who come from Beirut.
· They grow up with shooting in Beirut.
· Did they kill him?
· No, they just wounded him.
· They should have killed him.
· What are you saying? Do you know what you're saying?
· Of course I know what I'm saying.
· What good is it to kill the poor man?
· He's not a poor man, he's a Moslem.
· He doesn't know what happened. He wasn't even born then.
· Then he should know. They should all know.
· She's right, something must be done. Too many years have gone by and nothing has been done.
· What do you want to be done?
· I want them to admit what they did.
· What for?
· So everyone knows.
· So everyone knows, so what?
· So then it's a beginning. They can begin to pay us back.
· How are they going to pay us back?
· I don't care if they pay us back or not, as long as they know.
· My granddaughter knows. She wants to join the underground.
· Does she want to shoot diplomats?
· She wants to fight for her race.
· She just wants to fight.

· No, she grew up with the stories.

· Who told her those stories? What kind of stories are they for children?

· They like to hear those kinds of stories. The Jews play their stories over and over again.

· They're our stories. Our grandchildren should know them.

· So they can hate and kill?

· Not to hate and kill. To know where they come from.

· They come from television.

· They all come from killing and sex.

· Not all of them.

· All of them and all of us. We all come from killing and sex.

She Was Someone Else

The kids weren't to know, no one was to know.

"Zeke, no one must know, Charlie couldn't bear it if anyone knew."

She was thirty years old and wanted to get out of the life she had built and yet she was afraid. Meanwhile the one she turned to for escape wanted to stand on the fire-escape and shout to everyone that he loved her, he loved her.

He walked the streets delirious and loved everyone and everything through his love for her. He wanted to be with her all the time or at least for a night for they were never together for longer than a moment and Carmella next door was always dropping by.

"Zeke, you here again?"

He wanted to sleep with her without getting up and worrying that Luigi would know. He wanted to wake with her in the morning and to hold her hand in the open and to eat pizza late at night with the door open and the gang dropping by for a slice. He wanted to taste what he envied others having for so many years. Every fiber of his life seemed charged with her voice and her odor and all the years of wandering seemed to come to an end. He wanted to devote the rest of his life to being with her.

But she panicked. Like a rabbit in a headlight she froze with fear and all their passion became a fever in which even the days were like a sleepless night and none of them passed without the ghosts of guilt.

"Charlie will want to kill me."

Charlie? Old Charlie who was the father of her children and would always be?

"I'll talk with him."

"Oh, Zeke, don't be crazy."

"We'll talk with him together. It will all work out somehow."

"Oh, Zeke, you don't know him at all."

Not know him? Not know Charlie after all those years?

"It'll work out, Dolores, we all love each other."

"Oh, Zeke, you're so blind."

You came back but not as old Charlie a friend once knew. You were someone else not even you could know, a stranger buried under your shell and now breaking through with hatred and rage.

"Zeke, you shouldn't have called me at the hospital."

"But you never called."

"I can't talk with you now."

"What's happening, what's going on?"

"I don't know what's going on."

"But what about Charlie?"

"Charlie? All Charlie wants is to question me every night. He wants to know every detail, where, when, how, everything, and then he wants to kill me."

"I'll go see him."

"He doesn't want to see you. He hates you."

"He hates me."

"Well, what did you expect?"

Your voice over the phone was like a tape recording in a corpse.

"You can come over if you want. Dolores is working and I'll be home with the kids."

You read to Luigi and held Mimi in your arms as if they would prevent anything from changing. After they were in bed you talked as if nothing had happened.

"Dolores and I love each other. What happened is unimportant."

But under your shell you looked sick to the one who wanted to hug you and tell you that he was also sick, he was also burning with a fever.

You shrugged.

"Are you still going to California, Zeke?"

The nights were starting to cool and the mornings were cerulean and brisk. The trees were still green but in a few weeks they would blaze in another beautiful autumn. Luigi started school with excitement and new clothes and you both walked him there and back as if nothing had happened, but for the first time since he was an infant he started to pee in his bed.

She tried to hold onto herself in her role as a mother but she too had become someone else. In the zoo in the park she said that she too felt like she was in a cage.

"I feel as if he's hiding somewhere, he's supposed to be working but I feel as if he's watching me."

She was so frozen with pain she couldn't even cry.

"He's broken, Zeke. I may as well have killed him."

Mimi was fascinated by the gorilla and she screamed and waved as the other children bombarded him with peanut shells, the gorilla sitting in his tire like an old wino in full lotus and the shells bouncing off his armored chest.

"He says he wants a divorce."

A real peanut fell in the cage and he reached for it with his huge wrinkled finger and slipped it into his grimace and then spit out the shell and returned to his pose, his tiny eyes staring through the bars from deep beneath his heavy brow.

"My children are my life, I have no life without them."

The seal barked and waved her head from side to side and then plunged between the rocks.

"Then you're not coming to California?"

"How can you ask me that? Don't you see what has happened? Everything is destroyed. I've destroyed everything."

The polar bear stood up and then sank down and lumbered to his cave. The tiger paced back and forth and the elephant shuffled two steps back and two steps forward as if he were dancing.

"When are you leaving, Zeke? Are you leaving soon?"

Her voice was strangely like yours, the same inflection and strange resemblance that married people develop, the two of you fitting together like wheels of a clock, your separate wheels turning to catch each other's teeth, your children winding you tighter every day.

You were a jewel among men and now you would bleed with vengeance, and she whom everyone adored would shrink into deception.

Autumn splashed the city like a conflagration and never before did it feel so beautiful. The war vomited children without faces and yet never before did the world seem so alive. We all seemed together in a global burning and Guevara was murdered by those he would save, his deathface in a grotesque photo becoming the image of a saint.

Sex Education

· In my village the Moslem had a right to sleep with a Christian bride on the wedding night.

· But he never really did.

· Yes, he did. At least once anyway. I won't say her name but she had to go to his house and be deflowered by him before she could sleep with her husband.

- Those filth.
- Now there are no more virgins anyway.
- Now they don't even get married.
- They marry and they divorce and they marry and they divorce.
- Let them divorce. I would have divorced if I could have.
- You're not the only one.
- No, I loved my husband.
- I loved my husband too but I still would have divorced him.
- I was married to mine six months before we slept together.
- How old were you?
- I was fifteen.
- Now they sleep with boys even before they're fifteen.
- It's better that way, let them learn fast.
- My great granddaughter knows more than I do and she's only thirteen.
- They teach it in school.
- That's good. Now they won't be jackasses like us.
- It won't make any difference. Everybody has to learn for themselves.
- I feel sorry for young people today.
- Everyone learns in their own way. We had our suffering and they have theirs.

She Begins To Wear Her Many Masks

"We were all squeezed in the car and I kept crying for my mother. The train took us to Beirut and then we went to an orphanage in the hills above. But it was not really an orphanage, it was really a prison and they made us bow and beat us if we did not learn their prayers. Food? What food? There was no food, some hot water with a little flour mixed in. The other children? They are shadows to me now. It is all a dream to me now. Even my mother is like a dream. I don't know if she was real or not."

She becomes a girl again. She becomes her daughter and their figures dissolve into each other in the blur that wants to come clear.

"I wish I knew what I looked like when I was a child. I wish I had just one photograph or drawing of my childhood. I must have been strong. I fell sick and they left me to die with the other sick children but I did not die. I got well and joined the others in the prison-orphanage. I must have been strong because there was nothing to eat. Twice a day we gathered for the hot water with a little flour mixed in and then afterwards we stood outside the Moslem's window and waited for him to throw away the orange rinds from his dessert. I don't remember everything but I never forget those spiralled rinds we picked from the ground and gnawed like vermin."

She is the eternal girl becoming a woman in the waves of history, the venus who rises from the foam and crash of severed genitals, her arms up and her breasts open, the gale and spray her diaphane.

"I guess we were there for about three years before the Moslems left. You can read the books and find out. Then one day we heard bombs and they exploded all around us and we hid under our beds. We lay there and when all was quiet we came out and peeked through the halls. They were empty. The Moslem was not there anymore. He was gone. Then strange soldiers came and they were speaking French. First the French and then the English. I remember they taught us Christmas songs in English. I remember the Christmas when the boxes came from the Red Cross. Combs and brushes and shoes and stockings. We were not children anymore and we wanted mirrors to shape our hair."

She is her daughter now, the girl in the dark past of a mother without an image.

"Not too long afterwards a rich merchant, one of our people who lived in Beirut and was not touched by the massacre, came to the orphanage to adopt one of us. He called me daughter and took me to his family but I did not become one of them. I was to eat with the other servant who was an orphan like myself only older. I stayed there two years before I ran away. My blood came during that time. I was hanging the wash on the line and felt it flow down my leg. Berjouhi, the other girl, told me what it was and how to wear a cloth for it. It was Berjouhi who told me to escape or I would stay a servant like herself. 'Don't stay here,' she said, 'don't let yourself become like me.' Poor thing, she was not too attractive, to tell the truth, but so good and kind. 'Go,' she said, 'there is a woman in town who is looking for a wife for her son in America.'"

She begins to wear her many masks.

The first one comes in a little passport photo of a fifteen year old girl with a bow in her collar. She stares back at the black cowl and does not smile at the puff of light, her almond eyes and dark hair like an exquisite portrait by a master.

"We were supposed to stay on the lower deck of the ship but I used to go above and stare at the first class. No, I didn't envy them, I just stared and admired their clothes. I had a good time on that ship. Everyone else got sick so I got to eat their food. And when they were well we sang and danced. You remember old Antranig on Highpoint Avenue? He was on that ship with me and he had his oud with him and we all sang and danced. I enjoyed that voyage even though I was lost."

Loneliness and Gossip

· I got a call from Zevart the other day.
· How is she
· She's miserable. She can't take the loneliness.
· She has to take it.
· What else is she going to do?
· She can move in with her children.
· Would you move in with your children?
· I can deal with the loneliness.
· People die from loneliness.
· Zevart's not going to die from it.
· It's only a few hours at night. During the day she can keep busy.
· We're not the only ones who are lonely. The young are lonely too.
· My nephew is lonelier than I am.
· Your nephew doesn't have to be lonely. He can find someone.
· We can find someone too.
· I can't live with anyone anymore.
· I can't even live with my children anymore.
· I visit them and they sit in their den watching television.
· No one talks anymore. They all watch television.
· I'm glad. I used to hate all that talking. Everybody talking about each other.
· The television gossips even more.
· The television is all gossip. Even the news is gossip.
· I like gossip. It keeps us together.

She Is Called California

When we were kids we used to watch the sunset from on top of the road that snaked down into the marshes of Secaucus. The road would disappear out of sight into the cattails of the garbage dumps and on the other side of the marshes lay the blue hills of the horizon.

The image of America always seemed to be on the other side of those hills, a kind of motherland that waited to be explored. As the road snaked down and got lost in the marshes it seemed to point toward manhood and one day we would follow it.

It was our rite of passage and the tunnels of Pennsylvania were like a birth canal. It led to exotic names like Wheeling and Columbus and our excitement was like an instinct that kept pushing us forward, each of us thumbing our way into the darkness and testing ourselves against the unknown. Keep going, it said, don't stop, get a trucker at a cafe in the middle of the night and make St. Louis by dawn, the sudden thrill of the Mississippi and the new Memorial Arch shining in the long rays of the sunrise behind us, the great Saarinen line like a crowning into that immensity called America and the belly of the west.

But there was no America, there was nowhere that could be named and the road pushed through a history of massacres and a cemetary of another culture. There was only the land and she had no name and she grew more beautiful as the road continued across the plains and the Rockies. What would she be like on the other side of the desert?

All right, let her be called California, the word itself like a woman, her great thighs accepting anyone and her winters always green, her gentle hills like a boy's first whore with a gold tooth in her smile.

The first time he entered her he felt he had arrived at the end of a journey and he stayed as long as he could. And though the journey never ended and continued to foreign cities and museums, somewhere inside him always wanted to return.

And so he returned and settled in a cabin by the sea, her deer prancing through the high grass and her raccoon staring over the garbage can, her blue heron nesting in the canyon and then gliding like a paper kite across the lagoon, her egret poised in the low tide and her hills darkened with redwood and madrone, her clouds over Bolinas Bay and her wildflowers by the little Van Gogh cabin that rented for only seventy-five a month and all his watercolors filling with her vulvas and her breasts.

All his love of nudes went into her shores and he wanted to fuck her with his brush. She became the image for his longing and like any nude she could be terrible and full of pain.

There were only a few others on the mesa in those days and the loneliness was often so painful he wanted to die. The leaves of the eucalyptus were like daggers in the grisly fog on his way to town every afternoon and the post box empty until a letter came from Leo.

"Hey, Zeke, what's it like out there? We're coming too, me, Charlie, all of us. The rents and the roaches have done us in."

Two more families joining the centuries of migration, your vans puttering across the wilderness of hippy-hating rednecks. You stopped outside Reno where Tony was dealing blackjack on the weekends and fishing the rest of the time. He said anyone who went to California was nuts. He said it was becoming another shit hole and you should stay in the desert.

"You can have California and shove it up your ass."

By the time you arrived all the flower children were gone and all the runaways and drunks were littered in Golden Gate Park like refugees from the murderous suburbs. The newspapers were full of bloody

faces from Chicago and there were riots in Berkeley and Oakland.
You looked for a quiet place with a good school for the kids and yet
you didn't want to be away from the action.

By the end of summer the hills were so dry the deer came looking
for water by the cabins. The mice chewed the roots of the queen anne's
lace and the dry stalks toppled into the long parched grass. Then as
usual the rains came around Halloween and the seabirds started to
arrive on their way south, the merganser and pintail and bufflehead,
the petral circling in the shallows and the pelican gliding with huge
majestic wings. They were like angels, the cousins of the chicken we
treat like shit.

A lonely artist went to watch them and tried to hold on to the
musselled rocks and the mesmeric anemones of the tide pools. He
longed for his place in the earth and a natural life but it seemed impossible without people and money. He had none left and went back
to the streetlights where he found a job at the Post Office in Berkeley.

The Woman With The Naked Breast

In the dark mornings down in the basement of the Post Office there
was an old black World War Two veteran who stood by the wall and
hummed old jazz tunes while he smoked his pipe and shuffled his
letters. He was not really old but his tobacco and his Ellington songs
seemed to purl from another age in the golden years.

Nixon was just elected and the war raged on, but though there was
tension between the straights and the longhairs the old black vet with
the kinky white sideburns stood by the wall in his separate world and
shuffled his mail as if he were enveloped in a cloud of aromatic tobacco smoke, his letters tapping in rhythm to his songs from Tin Pan
Alley.

What cancer or transfer awaited him he didn't know, he just cased
his mail and went for his eggs in the cafe on Shattuck Avenue and
then continued with his route in the hills.

His face becomes the image of early mornings and the good feeling
of being warm inside with the rest of the gang, of the world of our
childhood when we were paperboys together, a boy waking in the
darkness and catching the alarm just before it went off so it wouldn't
wake his mother.

He would hold his shoes and walk in his socks past her bed into the kitchen and turn on the old four-legged oven and stand by the flames until the water boiled. Instant coffee had just come out. Big Richie was the one who discovered it.

"It's good, Zekey. Ya gist put hot warta init wid lotsa shuga an milk. It's called Instin Maxwell House."

Good to the last drop, said the empty cup in the old Lyondekker illustration. He would drink it with a chunk of *choreg* and then tiptoe down the stairs and try not to wake old Mrs. Barbalinardo who'd be up anyway. Then he'd run to be with the gang in the empty storefront and Big Richie the manager would always be yelling like a foreman in a post office twenty years later.

On Wednesdays and Thursdays the paper had to be shuffled together and everyone had to get to the office early for a place on the tables and sometimes there would be a fight for it, Big Richie shoving his way in between with his big jelly belly and getting his glasses knocked off from the flying fists, good old Richie, dear Richie whom everyone made fun of, wherever he is now, his ashes in the wind.

Sometimes those who had to wait for a place on the tables would go down the street to the bakery and buy hot buns from the old flour-dusted baker who was their comrade of the dark morning when everyone else was asleep, and then they would all feast on the buns and the turnovers with their lips and noses powdered with sugar and smeared with milk and their hands black from the fresh ink.

And when they finished shuffling the papers they would hang around the tables and twist them into flips, each kid checking the other's as if the long phallic rolls they stuffed into their canvas bags were some kind of weapon or ammunition. Flip after flip in the odor of paper and kerosene and the warmth of being inside and telling puerile jokes more archetypal than lurid, like the one about the little creature who gets caught in a woman's hole with a big monster coming in and whitewashing the walls.

And when everyone was finished they would slowly enter the streets that were dark in winter and rose-tinted in the spring and each boy would be alone with his heavy bag that he balanced on his back like a coolie or a hero, depending on his mood.

And he would trudge through the morning weather and bring news to the tribe of grown-ups in the different halls and vestibules, each with its own special odor and a mystery behind the door, the different characters and scenes he would peek into when he went to collect.

And he would stop to rest and sit down to read the comics in one of the fancy vestibules with a rug and everywhere would be charged with the power of the dawn and the profound silence of being awake while everyone else was asleep.

He loved walking in that silence and listening to the sparrows and pigeons, and then one morning came the shock of the woman with the naked breast, her nipple and areola exploding his eyes like a blinding flash when she suddenly opened the door to get the milk and her robe opened as she bent to pick it up. And when she saw that she was not alone she covered herself and smiled as if she did not have to be embarrassed or have anything to fear from the downy-faced boy wearing his cousin Aram's old woolen army hat and the fatigue jacket that was too big for him so he had to roll the sleeves.

And she was right. For though her breast would fix in his memory and never fade or change, he still lived in that world where beautiful women were only kissed or hugged and she was more vision than woman. She was almost the morning itself and how it glowed in a veil more shadow than light and he tried to hold on to the soft fugitive colors of her open robe as if they were the seeds of all the nudes to follow, her emanation more powerful than the body she prized while he walked on as if in a stream of a throbbing epiphany and wanted more of her, to embrace her and release the overwhelming waves that surged through his limbs and would later become so painful.

He kept hoping she would come out again and she began to appear in other places, less a figure than the glowing bricks and poles that would one day blacken, bend and crumble in the warp of time, her swirling veil blazing and searing his eyes in the wound of adolescence and masturbation.

He walked on and finished his route with the sun rising behind the skyscrapers across the river, the long golden ray like a spear in his eyes.

When he got home his mother would be leaving for work. She would be at the factory all day and once a week he would go there in the afternoon and sweep the floor and clean the ladies room.

The International Lady of the Garment

She walks jauntily and eager to get ahead in the world, to buy new curtains and a kitchen set. She comes from another country, her genes knotted to who knows where in the web of rape and plunder.

She shakes her hair and breathes deep. No flowers on the way, no rice paddy or sugar cane, but the same sun rolls a golden carpet past the garbage can and the bum snoring on the stoop.

She takes her seat by the piles of cloth, fifteen women at each side of the row, face down and arms forward, right knee to the incessant whirr.

Whirr of fashion, whirr of profit, whirr of work for rent and food. Hour after hour with the pressers in their undershirts sweating in the steam, the boss in the office arguing with the jobber, the floors littered with balls of dust and thread and pennant scraps, the cracks between the boards filled with pins, the worn wood stained with oil, everywhere grimy with oil and dust and everyone together in the loud whirr like insects in a hive.

She gossips and giggles, yawns and sighs, picks her nose and bends back to her pattern and her stitch, her fingers fluttering to fold and smoothen the unruly cloth.

This week taffeta, last week wool, the next bright jersey or chiffon. On painted models who pose with a rifle or a donkey in the desert. For the poor to gaze at and the rich to throw away. With fluff or piping, checkered or striped, multi-colored in the endless styles for vanity and parade. They are sold and worn in the world across the river but any fool can sew the pieces in place.

Yet she is no fool. If she could speak the language, if she were born here . . . but she couldn't and wasn't and would be either fool or corpse in a river or desert, machine-gunned or starved by the same perversion that rules her pay, the vast design of the endless greed that hides inside the glamour and the profit.

She looks nothing like a model with her back bent and her face down, a kerchief around her hair to keep the dust off, a dusty apron over her bosom. She doesn't raise her head until lunchtime.

Leftovers from last night's dinner she warms on the presser's steam. She rests in the peace and quiet, the noise now an echo in her head. She chats with her friend while the others babble in their own language. They share years and weariness and yet only at Christmas do they spend an afternoon together with the grab-bag and the cake.

They work not by the hour but the dress and she pushes herself for the extra tag while she's still young. Later in the afternoon the boy comes from school. He used to come to visit his mother in the next seat but now the boss has hired him to sweep the floor and clean the ladies room. He always stares at her. His mother has been working at these machines longer than she herself has been alive. Will she also be here in her middle-age, her teeth gone and a son to support, her breasts fallen and her hair grey?

She lifts her feet for his broom as he sweeps around her chair.

She catches him staring at her again from the other end of the machines.

Staring as he stared into the old brown photographs of a mother he had never seen before, her strange youth shuffled with the dead in the Dutch Masters cigar box. He would pull it from the closet and study her as if she were alien.

Was that her, the heavy illiterate he yelled at when dinner wasn't perfect? Was his mother also a beautiful woman like the lace-maker of Vermeer, her eyes downcast as she curled her fingers in a nacred light?

He never tired of her story as if she were another venus in a personal form.

"I was off the boat and behind the machine in the same week. Not yet sixteen and my breasts still growing. Twelve hours a day, six days a week, no benefits, no complaints. For Tahan the Syrian, sewing handkerchiefs."

No photograph of the factory and the only pictures are of Sundays at Lake Hopatcong and the picnics at Woodbridge, young immigrants the age of college kids laughing on their day off. She's one of them, dark and mysterious. Not the storyteller so vivid and real with her garlic breath and false teeth, but the sepia image with oriental eyes and a strange smile.

"Kerchief after kerchief, how many kerchiefs in nine years? For less than they make now in Chinatown. I learned no English but my Arabic improved. No one needed English when the neighborhoods were full of us. No radio, no television, no phonograph or tapedeck and only a Charlie Chaplin for those of us who could read. But every

Sunday was a crowd when we used to pile into Sahag's dry-cleaning truck and head for Lake Hopatcong or the woods of Woodbridge.

In one photograph she's fooling around and posing like a dame in a Gainsborough portrait, her left foot arched and her young fingers in a royal gesture. In another she's gay and vivacious like a Fragonard girl on a swing and in yet another she's serious like an Ingres, the moody young woman who is beginning to love her breasts and is made to feel ashamed of them.

"We were in factories all day and at night we were packed together in the coldwater flats with a couch in the kitchen and a common toilet in the hall. My husband was a stranger and I turned my face and let it happen. It could have been worse. Many of us were not virgins when we came."

She stares at the big box camera like an imitation of Leonardo, *La Belle Ferronière* with a line between her lips not a smile or a frown.

"*Kef?*" Sure, there was a lot of *kef*. There was Chubby Rubin with his oud and Jack-knife Nishan with his clarinet and Highball Khosrof slapping his dumbag. We made *kef* as much as we could. We were young, we were full of life, we survived. Lucina herself, rest her soul, could play the oud as well as any man, but she rarely played for us because it was shameful for women to be artists in those days. Her son now curses the old crones who killed her fingers but that's how we lived then, there was *kef* but with rules. We lived in each other's eyes. Families were strong and yet the time would come when brothers would hate each other over a few dollars or an argument. There was *kef* and there was hatred, just like today, and the good times were like water in a desert. Most of the time we were all buried behind a needle or a cloud of steam."

The cameras improve and lose their sepia tint and meanwhile she matures. She's in her late twenties and is full-bodied and strong like a Titian or a Courbet, her shyness and vanity overcome by her love for the child she holds at her breast.

"Your brother was born just before the Depression. I was on my way to the bathhouse and got as far as the stables when my water broke. Ice-block Harry had just finished his route and he rode me home in his horse-cart. That was a Friday afternoon. Your brother wasn't born until Saturday morning. I lay in the back room and suffered while life went on as usual, Mano the baker delivering bread and the old women jabbering in the kitchen just like any other day. Happy? Of course I was happy, your brother was fat and healthy and covered with silver and sugared almonds. But two weeks later I was in the factory and my mother-in-law was carrying him there to be nursed. I would stop work and give him my breast and then go back to the machine. He drank no milk but my own for two years and meanwhile the kerchiefs had become kimonas, the boss now Zorab, another Syrian. I was lucky to work when others had no jobs, but my youth disappeared through the eye of a needle. Then the union started. What do I think of the union? I kiss their feet. Wouldn't you for two days off and only eight hours a day? It was around that time I married your father and a little while later I started making dresses with the Italians on Highpoint Avenue. That's when I started learning English, at least the kind those Italians spoke. You were born soon after. Your father was poor from the Depression and I paid for your birth myself. Your cradle was a laundry basket but we were happy until your father got sick."

She's in her middle-thirties and still capable of starting a fire in the eyes of lust, but in the photo of her posing with her family on the back roof, the washline filled with sheets and a clothespin in her fingers, the venus has become a Degas in his later years when his women put on weight, her hair pinned back and her chunky body in a housedress.

"After your father got sick I did alteration work at home until you were old enough for school. Whatever money was left after the rent and food all went to the doctors and the quacks until he died. Those were the hardest years and I went from factory to factory with my scissors and my shuttle and the little pillow for the chair. All I cared about was that my seat was by a window and a fresh breeze."

Color has arrived but it's crude and her flesh looks unnatural in the photo from the commercial studio on the avenue. The photographer has her holding back her smile, perhaps to hide the bridge in her teeth, and she's looking up as if at the clouds, her hair curled by a permanent and her dress seamed with those shoulder pads of the war years. His imitation of art is pathetic and her vitality smothered by his commercial goals, yet somehow her spirit survives and there is a glow in her eyes despite the touch-up.

She has become like that old faded print of Rembrandt's *Woman Bathing* that hung on the wall of cousin Aram's funky woodstove living room. Aram was never one for interior decoration and that

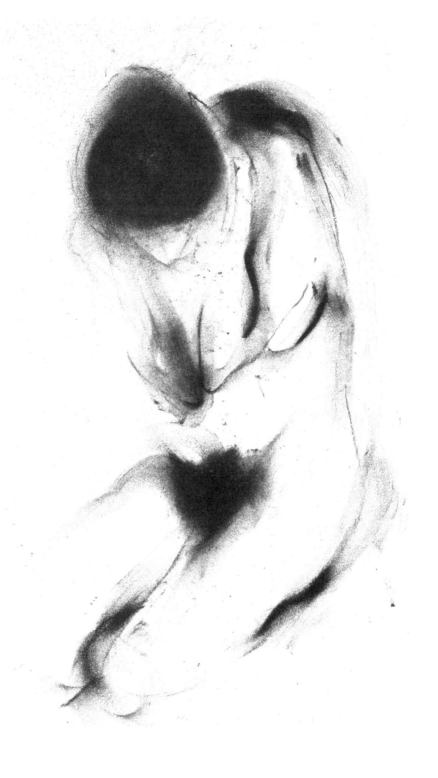

cheap little print stayed in the same spot for ten years, a child staring at it year after year until one year he was tall enough to look straight at the darkness between the thighs of the little woman who lifted her dress and stood in the shallow water.

Who was she? Who was that little woman with the darkness between her thighs and her face in shadows? She reminded him of his mother, she had the same strong thighs and graceful hands, her head bowed as if praising the water. She seemed to be stepping out of the darkness into the glowing water like a morning vision from the realm of dreams, her face half-hidden by the shadows of the past. She was not only like his mother but someone further back, an ancient figure that waited for her face to come to view. She was waiting for him to paint her in his own way. He would have to study her and all the other masters until he could paint his own glow in the darkness, he would have to keep staring and drawing until he could paint his own lady with a garment in her hands.

She keeps on sewing.

She laughs bright teeth that will turn to porcelain before the next war. The boy stares at her again and she wonders what his erections are like. Her fiancé's in Japan and away from the danger in Korea. He sent her a quilt from Tokyo with an embroidered dragon on luminous silk. How much was the Japanese operator paid to sew it?

She sews until the bell rings and the machines drone to a quiet.

The elevator man waits until the car is full and he listens to the gossip. His clothes are tattered and his face unshaven like a bum, but she's never seen him drunk. Maybe he's demented or shell-shocked or living out his years in the gloom and dust because he doesn't know what else to do. Or maybe he's an artist who can't find any other work.

He carries them up and down, up and down, his international ladies of all different ages.

The old freight elevator passes the signs of the other shops as if it is slowly sinking down the layers of history. *Carmen. Young Bess. Lily of France. Sophia.*

The low sun sends another carpet of gold for her heels clicking on the sidewalk. She will stop at the bakery on her way home and buy some *cannelli* for dessert. The dying light is glorious and everywhere is bathed with colored shadows. Now here in another city. Once more through the ages.

America

· I wonder what I would have become if I was born in this country.
· You would have been a movie star.
· You think so?
· Sure, why not? Your nose is too big but they can fix that.
· No one's going to fix this nose. This is my father's nose.
· I wonder if I could have been a big shot if I were born here.
· You already are a big shot.
· Remember that Persian Lamb coat she had? Only big shots wore those coats.
· No, I mean a big shot like Eleanor Roosevelt.
· Eleanor Roosevelt was a miserable woman.
· How do you know?
· I heard it on the television.
· All I want is health.
· Oh you and your health. You have to enjoy yourself too.
· The only enjoyment I know is my children.
· You see them once a year.
· They're too busy worrying about how to have a good time.
· They have so much and still they're miserable.
· It's a shame the way they live now.
· If everyone lived like you we'd still be in the village.
· What's wrong with the village?
· I like it better here.
· I go to Las Vegas, I go to Tahoe, who wants to go back to the village?
· It was like a village when I first came to this country.
· Where you talking about?
· In Binghamton, New York. My cousin had a farm there.
· I didn't know any Binghamton. Not a week after Ellis Island I was in the factory. Oh, America, everyone said on the boat, as if we were going to heaven.
· That's what Pinocle Nishan said on the boat. He said, "Do you think I'm going to America to work?"
· He was a gambler.
· He had a cafe.
· It's the same thing.

· My husband used to play cards there all night.

· All the boys did.

· I used to complain, but what else were they going to do, sit in the kitchen?

· My mother-in-law's kitchen was always full.

· That's because she made *arak* in the bathtub.

· I used to hate it. I can still smell the stink of those raisins in the barrel.

· People came all the way from Paterson to buy her stuff.

· She had a good idea. Maybe I should make *arak* in my bathtub and then my kitchen will be full at night.

· You need more than *arak* to fill your kitchen with people.

· I don't want mine full. I can hardly keep it clean.

· My house is too big for me to clean.

· We should all live in our garages.

· I lived with my husband and four children in an apartment that was not half the size of the house I live alone in now.

She Becomes Terrible

From the Berkeley hills the Golden Gate is the vanishing point in a landscape of the sundown and by mid-winter the sun, setting further and further north again, floats for a moment like a ball in a cradle between the pylons of the bridge, Alcatraz Island like a stepping stone to its death behind the horizon, the bay like a clean slate on a crisp afternoon at the end of a rain.

Winter is the best time for blossoms in Berkeley and everywhere seems pink and yellow from all the plum trees and abundant broom. That winter they seemed especially prolific and one afternoon some political people were organizing to make a park out of a muddy lot that belonged to the university. Suddenly, while stopping to watch them, there came a voice from the sidewalk. It was Dolores.

"Do you like being a mailman, Zeke?"

Her eyes were the same, her voice was the same, and yet her smile was alien.

"You must enjoy it. You always said you wanted to wake up early instead of sleeping late."

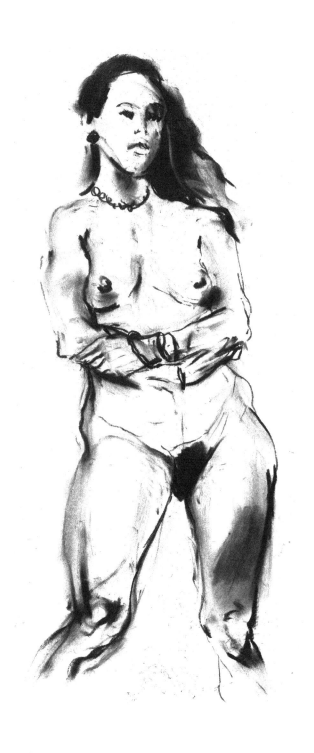

She was not really Dolores. She was like an alien who was acting friendly.

"Why are you talking to me like this Dolores? I haven't heard from you in a year and you talk to me as if you were an alien acting friendly."

Her face grew hard and she began to grow snakes in her hair, a gorgon whose deadly silence was like a knife in the eyes. She was so raw with pain she became cold as if to numb herself, but the one she used to call her brother was too blind to see beneath her mask. He wanted to hold her and transform her and threatened by his need she turned away and disappeared, more phantom now than woman with her hair down her back and her buttocks in the loose skirt like knives opening a wound that never healed.

She was not Dolores anymore. She was the woman who said no, the medusa with no face, her void like a blight on the kingdom of visions. She was the woman with a head on a platter like a bloody phallus, the scissor woman who disappeared with all the hair.

The rains finished by Easter time and the hills were vibrant with new grass. The park was full of flowers and children and it was called *People's Park*, a vision of everyone together as if there were no private property.

But there is private property and everyone defends their own space, the war raging and the flowers blooming like demarcations for a battle zone.

After finishing the route there would be a few minutes for hanging out in the basement and sometimes Jackpot the maintenance man would be down there. He would have his feet on the bench and he would be drinking a cup of hot chemicals from the soup machine.

"How's the paintin, Zeke?"

His big smile and his white cotton socks were like old Mr. Ferroluzzi's, the janitor in grammar school who seemed to live in the boiler room with his cat and the flames.

"What you paintin deez days? You paintin any nudies?"

He seemed untouched by the war or the waves of junk mail that flooded the bins like sewage from a voracious market. He seemed to live in the basement like old Mr. Ferroluzzi sitting in his rocking chair with the cat in his lap. He sucked his toothpick and screwed his finger in his ear and his smile seemed to come from somewhere in a boiler room that was always warm in winter and cool in the summertime and was never touched by principals and rules. He was the old man in the basement who loved to talk about nudes.

"I love nudies."

The nights passed with beer and tobacco and the days working hard. A cat came to live in the shack and began modelling on the rocking chair, her belly rising in peaceful waves. Then one night there was a knock on the door.

"Zeke, I'm so miserable. I'm so miserable, Zeke."

Her throat was locked and she could hardly breathe. She said you were even worse. She talked about your drinking and her numbness, each making the other worse. She sat in the rocking chair and cried and all her confidante did was to want her again. Her cold and stony mask had transformed into a tragic queen's and she was beautiful again.

But the worms of distrust had started to feed. Distrust, hatred, guilt and pride, the worms buried in our wounds that would keep some of us apart for the rest of our lives, Leo moving to Wisconsin and not wanting anything to do with the past, Tony in Nevada not wanting anything to do with Leo, Shlomo in New Mexico trying to start a new life.

Spring was over by the end of April and the tall grass began to dry. The park did not belong to the *people*, it belonged to *the university*, whatever those names meant, one represented by blind and angry rebels and the other by blind and fearful bureaucrats.

The outrage of the war became a wild excitement and the streets filled with the bayonets of a bewildered national guard, the helicopters hovering above and dropping tear gas.

One young man was killed. Another blinded.

The decade of our youth was over.

In a chapel just two blocks from the park a chorus of pubescent boys and girls tried their best to sing for the young man who died, the music flowing through the centuries in their off-pitch and broken voices, the glorious requiem Mozart wrote for himself and never finished.

Rugs

· Annahid's unhappy because of her breast operation.

· The television says those operations aren't needed anymore.

· Doctors like to cut breasts off.

· Only those who don't like women.

· Only those who don't like women become women doctors.

· I don't know, my doctor is a good boy and he cut both mine off.

· Annahid's depressed about it. She's still young, she's only sixty.

· She reminds me of Arpi, rest her soul. She was always worried about how she looked. Even on her deathbed she had to sugar her face. "I can't help it," she said, "I need to look good." There she was dying and she had to sugar her hair off from her face.

· My mustache is so thick I could shave it.

· Don't shave it, you'll look like a man.

· I already look like a man.

· I don't care what I look like anymore.

· No, I want to look good.

· What look good? How can we look good with these faces?

· A face is like a good rug. The more it's stepped on the better it shines.

· They don't make those kinds of rugs anymore.

· I sold my rugs.

· Those beautiful rugs?

· I'm not going to live forever. I sold them and gave the money to my children.

· They should have taken the rugs instead.

· They don't want them. They like wall to wall.

· Everyone has wall to wall.

· I'm going to have it too, it's easy to keep clean.

· How much did you sell them for?

· Five thousand. Three for the big one and two for the small ones.

· I remember when you bought them from Hightone Toomas, the importer. How much were they then, two hundred?

· That was forty years ago.

· What forty? Sixty not forty, sixty.

· Sixty, forty, what's the difference?

· They don't make them anymore. Even on the other side they make them by machines now.

· Who cares, I'm going to sell mine too.

· They're too much trouble. I was always worrying about them being stolen.

· No, I'm keeping mine. They're full of memories.

· I don't want any memories.

· I've been looking at those patterns all these years now.

· So what, get rid of them.

· My son remembers them in the apartment back east. He says he loved that apartment.

· It was his childhood.

· It was a disgusting place. You had to work like a slave to keep it clean.

· I don't miss the east.

· I miss the people.

· They're all dead.

· Not all of them.

· Let them come here, I don't want to go back there.

· I call on the phone and Maritsa says, "It's costing you too much." Her son's a millionaire and she worries about a few dollars for the phone. I tell her, "Maritsa, I can afford a few dollars to talk to you."

· You can talk all day and it's not the same.

· I don't like the telephone, there's no taste in it.

· It's better than nothing.

· I'm going to fly back. I want to see them before they die.

· I don't fly anymore. What am I going to do, ask the girl to help me to the toilet like I was a baby?

· I was going to fly back to see Charcoal Armen but she died. I talked to her husband Arsen on the phone the other day. "Arsen!" I yelled so he could hear me. "You'll be all right! The winters will be hard but in the summer you can keep busy in the garden!"

· He'll be okay. He can visit the widows because he has a good name.

· So even if he didn't have a good name, what's he going to do at his age?

· You don't know, a man his age can still be active.

· On the talk show they said that if you have a good love life it never dies.

She Tries to Hold On But He Pulls Away

There's no blue box of Kotex in the closet anymore. She is very clean and he never saw any blood or even knew what the box was for. Now it's gone and they both begin to change at the same time, he with wet dreams and she with hot flashes.

He watches her with disgust.

"You look awful. Your dress is ugly, your hair is ugly, you look like a hag."

He wants her to look young and glamorous but her vanity has become a drop of spittle for her eyebrows and a pluck of hair above her lips. To be clean is most important and the advertisements are for someone else. Her hair doesn't need lustre and her teeth are half gone.

"And your breath stinks of garlic. Why don't you use tooth paste instead of baking soda?"

She knows he loves her and pays no attention to his changing moods, his chubbiness gone and his skinny limbs in an awkward slouch. She's home early from work one afternoon with some extra money. The piece work was good and she wants to buy him something special.

"Anything you want."

All right then, yes, there is something. A glove like Charlie's father bought for him in Tobler's Sportshop.

"But it's too expensive, Ma. It's twenty-four dollars."

"That's okay."

His father gone and his brother in the army, she turns to him for the meaning of her life; what else is she if not a mother?

He gives in and accepts the glove. Never before did he own anything so extravagant. He rubs it with neatsfoot oil every night and keeps it under his bed when he goes to sleep.

The new Little League has just started and Mr. Novato the coach recommends they soak their hands in the brine every night to make them hard. But it doesn't work and his hand hurts like a hero's from the fast ball that smacks loud in the palm, his fingers throbbing in the soft warm and oily leather as if in the dark hole of the cow herself.

He burns his name in the strap with the tool Mr. Massaro the shop teacher let him use during lunch hour. He slips it like a trophy on the end of the Louisville Slugger and joins the gang at the far end of the field while the big guys play on the diamond and when summer comes they play all day.

They strive and compete and when they're hungry they go to Tony's delicatessen for cold cuts on the fresh rolls. They chew and swish them down with soda pop and then sit on the stoop in the shade and argue about who's better, Rizzuto or Reese, Campanella or Yogi.

In the hot humid afternoons they get lazy and suck lemon ice from old Mr. Musso's pushcart with the beach umbrella. They lie in the grass and tell dirty jokes and make fun of each other. And as the days pass the oily glove becomes black with sweat and dirt and the drumming of his fist, his need to test his budding muscles and eager eyes, the soft leather and the deep pocket like a grail for the shiny white and red-seamed ball he longs to sail over the diamond and the crowd, over the wall and the rooftops as if it were his soul sailing into the sky until it was gone, gone beyond, gone utterly beyond.

But by the end of summer the glove is stolen. One afternoon Mr. Novato is teaching him and Charlie how to bunt and he leaves it on the bench and it disappears into the empty bleachers. Not only his name and his sweat and the shape of his hand but the twenty-four dollars and the afternoons he watched her behind the machine, a strand of hair stuck to her sweaty temple and her shoulders curved.

"I'm sorry, I'm so sorry."

"That's all right, you don't have to cry. When I save enough we can buy another one."

But he'll never take that much from her again.

"I don't want another one."

Her warmth has become too heavy and he struggles to tear it away. She laughs and has a good time with her friends in the parlor, the females cackling. Warm and generous Auntie Zaroohe and Aunty Zabel and Aunty Lucina now harpies and furies in oily lipstick and greasy rouge. They have become like the old fat woman on the bus who takes too much of the seat, the ugly female who stinks of perfume.

"You all talk so loud I can't sleep."

His brother never had any trouble sleeping. His brother will live with her until he marries, but this one wants to tear himself away and get lost in the cold and foreign streets.

One night he goes to watch the big guys play basketball in Hoboken and it's late when the varsity game is over. The buses don't come and he decides to walk up the viaduct in the fresh snow that began to fall in the afternoon. It has become deep and soft and there are no cars on the road. As he walks up the long bridge he can still smell the pleasant odor of the coffee roasting in the Maxwell House Factory and it mingles with the cold clean air.

The night is quiet and clear and he listens to the squeak of his galoshes in the powdery flakes. They glisten in the soft light of the old streetlamps and he peeks over his shoulder at his footmarks as if they are his name imprinted in the pure whiteness. Each step tastes delicious as if he's eating the snow while he plods up the bridge to where it enters the viaduct. At the end of the bridge he turns and looks down at the dark river and the jeweled lights of Manhattan.

He pretends he doesn't have to go back. He has his penknife in one pocket and thirty-five cents in the other. He can find a boxcar in the freight yard and sleep in the straw and in the morning he will be somewhere new. The night is soft and gentle and he wants to go to the other side of it. Already all by himself he has been to the other side of Hoboken and only last week he played hookey and took the bus to Manhattan and walked all the way up Fifth Avenue to the museum and no one could have possibly known he was there. The great pictures seemed to glow in the quiet galleries and he walked among them as if they were his fathers. He imagined living with them all the time. He would hide there and sleep with them in the darkness as if they were his totems. The pictures and the artists were the same and they would be his guides on the long journey ahead. He would be like them and suffer poverty and loneliness in order to paint.

As he looks across the river he nourishes the excitement growing inside him, the great city glittering under the drifting and luminous clouds. He will be an artist and go live in the bosom of art with all the other sons.

By the time he gets home he's exhausted and she has been waiting all the while.

"I've been worrying about you all night. Don't you care how painful it is for me to worry about you?"

The sheet is clean and fresh and curling under the quilt he fishes for a fantasy to lead him into sleep. As he drifts away he can hear her put his clothes with the dirty laundry and then go to her bed in the next room. He has stopped hugging her for several years. He used to lie with her sometimes and touch her breasts and snuggle in her warmth, but he doesn't want to anymore. The only hugs and kisses she gets now are with babies who can't resist. To have her son in the next room must be enough and there is always laundry to fill her arms.

Old Wool

· My son-in-law's father died and he gave me all his quilts. They were all dirty and I took the wool out and washed it but I don't feel like making more quilts.
· I'll help you. We can beat the wool in the sun just like the old days.

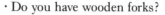

· Do you have wooden forks?
· We'll make some out of branches.
· That wool must be over a hundred years old by now.
· I still have all that we brought over on the boat.
· No one wants it anymore.
· They use goose feathers now.
· It'll be thrown away when we die.
· Of course, do you think anyone's going to wash it and beat it and sew it again?
· They throw away whatever's old and buy new stuff.
· It's better that way. Then no one will have anything to leave when they die.
· I sit at night and worry about what to do with all my junk. I worry about how to divide it equally and my children don't even want it.
· Don't fool yourself. When you die your grandchildren will come and fight over every little piece.
· We have to give everything away or the retirement home might get it.
· The retirement home got everything Arshaluce had. All her money and her house too.
· Did she take her quilt with her?
· They don't allow quilts in those places.
· When do you want to start on the wool?
· How about tomorrow?
· I'll come too but I can't sit on the ground like that anymore.
· Come and sit by us anyway.
· Good, we'll all sit together with Migurdich's wool, god rest his soul.

The Woman in the Lamborghini

In a smokey porno theatre some broken men sit hunched with their feet up and their knees drawn to their chests. They smoke and cough and staring up at the huge cunt on the screen they fuse in memory with the hard-ons we didn't know what to do with and stuck behind our belt with embarrassment, the afternoon behind Sal's garage when Big Richie had a black and white comic book of Dagwood with a hard-on and Blondie pointing to her bush, Big Richie rubbing his balls and rolling his eyes around. "Hey, Zekey, how come you can't draw like dis?"

The semen spurts across her face and she licks it like a gargoyle with a lolling tongue. *"Fuck me, you son of a bitch." "I'll fuck you, you cunt, I'll fuck you good."*

With bayonets and palette knives and her body slashed and left for dead, the hunger smothered with cigarettes or recycled by the military.

She spreads her legs and rubs her fingers, the vision now a whore with a price. How long can you keep your cock hard, buster? What have you made of your life? Artist? Don't give me any of that artist crap, you know what you can do with your art."

She sits at the bar and nods hello, she advertises in the want-ads. *"Sexy kitten. Foxey Co-ed. My pointed firm nipples are waiting for you to cum all over them. Oriental Lady, if you can appreciate the finer things in life."*

She is the whore in the old Indian fable of King Asoka and the act of truth. She turned the river back, she performed an act of truth. *"What was it?"* he asks, *"what was your act of truth that turned the river back?" "Whoever comes to me,"* she says, *"whether he's hirsute or bald, whether he's a saint or a psychotic, an artist or a phoney, I treat him just the same, as long as he pays."*

She wants money. She wants a house in the hills and a bank account, otherwise get lost, buster, you know what you can do with your sketches. They go to the man in the orange vest and silver helmet, the dogs barking and the cats running up the tree. He feeds them to the roaring hole as if with oblations. More lines for the sea, our mother of garbage, more forests wiped away with our lust for a nude.

She is the woman in the Lamborghini, the mystery behind the

hundred dollar pair of sunglasses. She parks the car in a lot and with perfect poise walks across the street like an animal of prey, the rhythm of her buttocks so powerful you wonder what plan nature had in making her a sheik's wife, sheiks fighting sheiks to play with her nipples.

Then one day a drifter points a knife at her throat and says he will rape and kill her. She believes him. She accepts her death and a sudden calm overtakes her. She stares at him in the shadows and asks him why. "Why?" he yells, "Why have you said no all these years, why have you always turned away?" He rips her dress and as he mounts her he trembles and breathes violently. She looks up at his twisted and painful face and with her maternal instinct reaches to cradle it in her palms. "It's all right," she whispers gently, "you don't have to be angry anymore, you don't have to hate me." And with these words he bursts out crying, he can't stop crying, and she leaves him in the darkness and goes back home.

She Will Die

One day there was a face on a bench near Telegraph Avenue in the little green that was a memorial for the boy who died during the riots of People's Park.

"Hello, Zeke."

As if eleven years were but a moment, her voice still seductive. But what had happened to her face?

"What are you doing here?"

Her hands seemed swollen and her face an hallucination.

"I'm waiting for Mimi. We've been shopping. Here she comes up the street."

A strange young woman walked up to her mother like a colt in the awkward beauty of her youth, her hair long and shiny like her mother's used to be.

"Mimi, this is Zeke. He's an old friend."

Her sex quivered like blossom before fruit and as her mother beamed proudly she looked away from the old man who kept staring at her.

"I used to change uh I used to uh play with you when you were a child."

So what?

"Mama, I have to buy one more thing, I'll be right back."

She ran back to the young crowd and left a pair of eyes that wanted to hold on to her and make up for all the years since she was a child.

"Are you still painting, Zeke?"

"Of course, how could you ask me that?"

"Well, you could have stopped."

She talked about the divorce and the years it took, but she wanted to talk more about Luigi. He had been studying ecology but was switching to business because he was afraid of not getting a job. He liked rock music and fishing and hiking, little Huckleberry his parents worried over when they tried to figure out what to spoon into his life so he'd be happy. He was with you, Charlie, on a fishing trip. You had stopped drinking and had even started writing again.

She stared at something across the street, her eyes turning away in that familiar gesture that said she was going off into her own world for a while. It was only a moment but it was enough to study her face. There were follicle marks where the hair was plucked above her lips and the wrinkles were entrenched around them. Without her smile they became pathetic. She pursed her lips and the wrinkles grew deeper like an old dried apple the apple-man would transform into a hag.

He would carve those wrinkles even deeper and crouch like a wolf who would seek blood for all her years of silence. He would bare his teeth and pulling back his ears he would rip into her sagging neck and fallen jowl. Look, he would growl, look what has happened to all the years you were so beautiful. You're ugly now and I don't have to love you anymore.

But he was growling at himself, all the faces he clawed and slashed like a blind child desperate for the light. Where did it go? When would it come back?

A flock of sparrows chirped and peeped in the potted tree and then burst in the air and disappeared. The traffic roared and then died and then roared again in the awkward silence of nothing to talk about anymore. To the street people sprawled nearby the old couple may have seemed like friends or family but they were more like ghosts to each other as the names they once knew in common began to surface like bubbles in a foamy wake.

Then suddenly she smiled and the hag disappeared inside her dimples and the gap between her teeth. She was beautiful again but in a different way. There was a glow in her face like the one that comes after deep crying when the knots of hatred begin to loosen and love can flow through. It was her suffering. Not her melancholy and her easy tears but her suffering which was our suffering and the mess we made of our lives.

Soon Mimi would be gone and she didn't know what to do. She'd be back where she started when she was a teenager who became a nurse because what else was there to do?

"Maybe I'll go back to school. I'd like to be a midwife, but I don't know if that's really what I want."

What did she really want, the answer always delayed by her search for a man. She could paint, she could write, she always did envy artists who seems so self-absorbed and driven by their work. But that's not what she wanted. She wanted a home and a family and to do each day what had to be done to keep it. Alone in an affluent society she starved for a simple life while others starved for food and water.

"I'd like to go to the desert."

"Where?"

"To Nevada. Do you know Nevada, Zeke?"

"A little."

"It's beautiful, isn't it?"

"It's empty."

"That's what I like about it."

"What would you do there?"

"I don't know. I'd like to have a cafe."

She was off again on another fantasy of sagebrush and rabbits, the locals asking her for homemade eye-talian dishes. She would have another family of faded jeans and cotton kerchiefs, old corncobs and sweatstained leather, young hotrods and maybe some tourists taking the old road and everyone gathered at her tables like kinfolk. *Howdy, Dolorious, you comin to the community meetin tanight? I'll try but I got a lot of cooking to do.* She'd stop by later at the firehouse and chat with them. Then she'd walk home under the stars and smell the jasmine and in the morning she'd wake with the magpie and the lark. Mimi and Luigi would come for a weekend once in a while and they'd ride horses or sit by the creek and talk like friends and after they left she would miss them but she wouldn't be lonely. She would be alone with herself for the first time in her life and there would be no staring in the mirror or watching her weight. She would know herself and love would fill that place inside her where no man could ever reach. She would feel it stream through her limbs and she would become the old woman of the desert.

"How's your mother, Zeke?"

"She's old."

"She's not so old. I bet you feel older than she does."

She smiled and in its glow there came the vision of her death. She would die. In the snap of thumb and middle finger she would be hit by a virus or a cancer or a drunken kid overrunning a stop sign in a drag race. She would die like Nelly and no one would hear about it until months later. She would die in the desert and no one would find her body. She would be like one of those cadavers in the anatomy class with a beautiful young student sawing through her skull. She would be a pile of flesh an attendant fed to an incinerator and in the vision of her death she became more beautiful than she ever was in youth, each wrinkle a memory, each grey hair a moment of her grace and loveliness, dear Dolores who goes all the way back to a tiny kitchen in the village late at night, the gang getting stoned in the next room and her new friend, Zeke, drying the dishes as she put them away, his hand wanting to touch her but holding back and her hand reaching out spontaneously in a gentle stroke of affection like a sister's.

She turned and seeing Mimi approach she stood and brushed the seat of her trousers.

"I hope you can finish that painting your working on, Zeke."

She curled her arm around Mimi's shoulder and they turned to walk away.

"*Ciao,* Zeke. It's been so good to see you."

They walked up Dwight Way toward's People's Park. It had become a hangout for drifters, an abandoned field waiting for another generation to turn it into flowers. She stopped to shake a pebble from her shoe, her buttocks heavy and reminiscent of the soft globes of an ancient mother, mama and daughter walking past a photo of Reagan in the newspaper box, the future president staring from behind the bars with his hair the same as when he was boy as if he were mummified and preserved, little Ronnie, the eternal boy about to enter a term of blindness in the prison of history.

Oil and Fat

- There's a sale on olive oil in my supermarket.
- Buy me two gallons, I'll pay you back.
- My daughter says safflower oil is better.
- Now your daughter is an expert on oil too?
- First it's sugar and then meat and now they want to change the oil.
- They worry about their health.
- Let them worry about what comes out of their mouths.
- I like olive oil. I never use fat anymore.
- I like fat but I use butter in my *choreg* now.
- It's not the same. The old *choreg* with the fat had its own taste.
- Agavni still uses it but she doesn't tell anyone. She boils it and keeps it in her second refrigerator. Her son's a millionaire but he still likes fat in his *choreg*.
- I used to get it for a nickel a pound from the butcher.
- I used to get it for free.
- You can still get it cheap.
- No one wants to boil it anymore. They don't even know how.
- You don't have to know. You just throw an apple in and when it's brown the fat is ready.
- They say it gives you heart trouble.
- Everything gives you heart trouble if you sit on your ass all day.
- That's why they all run.
- My daughter gets depressed if she doesn't run.
- Your daughter looks like a skeleton already.
- She likes to look that way. It's the new style.
- Do men like it?
- They don't care what men like.
- Good for them.
- They don't get old so fast.
- What's wrong with getting old? So they look young, so what?
- So then they can go out and have a good time.
- Do they have to run to have a good time?

She's Not The Woman In The Dream Anymore

She's an old woman with a face like Sitting Bull's, her lips disappearing as she takes her teeth out and brushes them with baking soda.

She asks for a haircut in the backyard, she likes it short and comfortable.

"Zaykay, just cut it and don't be so artistic."

The white hairs blow in the wind like all the lines of all her portraits that never came out right, that always looked like someone else.

She takes a shower and sits in her burnoose and soaks her feet in a pan of water. And now come her toenails which are too hard for her.

"Some women pay a lot of money to have their toenails cut."

Less nail than fungal crust, chtonic and recyclable, her feet like the ground itself, the bunions and calluses like a transition into the world of rocks and trees.

"I'm going to make shish-kebab for our meal."

"I don't want any meat."

"It's not for you, it's for your brother."

"I'll eat the beans."

"Eat anything you want."

"I like beans."

"If you like beans I'll cook beans. If he likes meat I'll cook meat."

"What about you, what do you like?"

"I like whatever's leftover. I grew old on leftovers."

Orange peels, potato skins, bones and crusts, the portrait of her life a compost with wildflowers, the colors mixed in a protoplasmic swirl of slaughter and birth, blood red and death blue, blossom yellow to turn them into earth.

She clears the table while her sons talk about her bank account. She washes the dishes during probate and trusts. She sweeps the floor along with interests and taxes, her sons preparing for her death while she grows more alive each day.

The valley is home and she is back on her acre, her mother in the dawn and her father in the vines, her brothers in the fruit trees and the donkey in the compost.

She walks with her youngest son to his car as he holds a bag of her food in one hand and reaches with his other to hold her arm and kiss her face. She moves to check the bag and he grabs her breast instead.

It is beyond softness and feels universal, an old udder that could belong to any mammal. Never before has she been so beautiful who used to appear in dreams of rage. *Shut up! Leave me alone! I don't want it, take it back, I don't want your damn food!*

Those dreams have stopped and she's not a mother anymore. She's a little old woman who will die and who finally begins to emerge through the cataracts of a personal history. The once-a-month weekends with her now are wonders and her good health a treasure from whatever it is that keeps her alive.

She stands by the car and pats the hood as if it were a donkey.

"Are you afraid of dying, Ma?"

"No."

"You're not?"

"No, I'm not afraid of dying."

"Why, my son?"

"Because who will I talk with on Sunday mornings?"

"You can talk with God."

"I don't talk with God."

"Oh I always talk with God."

"You do."

"Oh sure."

"What do you say?"

"I say thank you, I always say thank you."

Paklava Alice in the Basement

· Let's go somewhere. Let's go to Oakland.

· Who's in Oakland?

· Paklava Alice is in Oakland. Her son just moved there and took her with him. I dreamt about her the other night.

· My goodness I haven't seen her in fifty years.

· The last time I saw her I bought paklava dough from her when she was making it in the basement. She would take some herself to the Italian and bake it in his oven and then her son would sell it. He was just a boy then. He used to take orders all over the neighborhood.

· She worked in the factory with me for a while before she started
making dough in the basement. I dreamt about her staying at home
with her family and I had to get up early and go to a factory. There
was no bus to the factory and I had to walk there. I was very frightened because I was so tired and my legs can't walk that far anymore.
Oh, what am I going to do, I said, I won't be able to get there and
then there will be no money to pay the rent. And then I woke up. Oh
God, thank you, I said, it was only a dream.
· What did it mean?
· It meant that she wanted to make dough in her basement instead of
going to the factory.

She Doesn't Give Up

No, she's not old Siranoush or Dolores or any of the others who
posed for the figure that never came clear, though each one shared
her gesture and her song. She is the one who never stops dying, the
eternal peasant of the vines who gives birth to history, her grandson
coming to age in the spasms of war and famine that reverberated in
his own rage and hunger.

Why life he cried, why more apples when they only rot in an abandoned field? Why me, Grandma, an old tree of unwanted apples
while lovely children starve in a desert? Is this why you planted and
reaped, this heap of a grandson who can't even see your face?

He wanted her, he wanted his grandmother as if she could bring
him back to the home he lost as a child. He thought he had found it
with all his godfathers in the world of art but they were all dead and
he wanted to join them.

It was over, *finito, kaput,* she would never come clear and he tried to
give up and never draw again. He wanted to die, he didn't want to go
on being the same old Zeke always wanting a woman whose face
kept changing.

But he could not die, his eyes never stopped and he felt like he lived
only so his hand could keep on doodling whether he was happy or
not. Give me a break, he cried, I need a vacation!

And so he went away as if he could find someone or become someone else. He went back to his youth and even further back to the land
of bones.

London, Venice and Rome A Generation Later

Soho, a porno market, and no more cabbage in Covent Garden, no
Charlie in the pub on Dean Street and the lanes were full of ghosts.
Yet, she was still there rubbing her neck in Degas' bathroom in the
Gallery, she was still lifting her gown in Rembrandt's pool, she was
still shaking her tambourine in Renoir's dance. There was no end to
her, the daffodils triumphant on the embankment and the same old
thrill from the curve in the Thames, Blake's *bar of gold*. *"As for myself,"* he said, *"I live by miracle."*

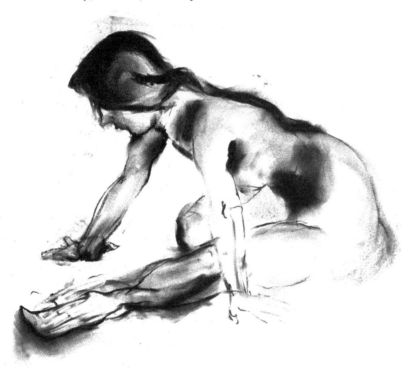

On the bus to Venice the swarthy drivers played loud Greek songs
and a King Crimson for the kids in the back. A ten gale wind blew
across the channel and some of the kids vomited in their bags, the ride
across Germany hard and sleepless but everyone determined to reach
the sun. A young woman sat in the seat across the aisle and as she tried
to sleep with her head in her hand the lovely curl of her nostril kept
flowing through the mountains to the cities of the dead.

Venice was a playground and a cemetary, a dead city of lovers and children and the rich and chtonic colors of bare brick and watermarks, flowerpots on the windowsills like Mrs. Belli's on Sip Street and the familiar laundry strung across the quiet canals, a bartender with gap teeth like Joe DiMaggio or old Mr. Tarquini the fish man with his bloody apron and his crushed ice, the fish eyes staring back as if they were still alive.

In the little Byzantine church of San Chrysostomo a middle-aged woman came in and lit a candle in the vault next to the one with the resplendent Bellini and the bald pilgrim beside her tried to join her prayer as the rhythmic click of feet in the lane outside kept rushing home to bread and soup.

Down through the boot of the continent he continued with his hunk of cheese and his *aqua minerale* on the *rapido sud*, a wave to Massacio in *Firenze* and Piero in the distant hills.

Down to Rome with her green horse in Michelangelo's Cordonata and Marcus Aurelius saluting in welcome. Come, pilgrim, he seemed to say, come sketch our graves and our women.

Another beggar girl to join the pile from India and Mexico, her palm open and her head askew as if her neck were broken.

Another lovely little girl in a red and blue polka dot dress and a black ribbon around her waist, her palm down and her hand on her hip as she stood in the piazza and cheerfully bounced her ball. *"Sesanta sei, sesanta sette, sesantotto, sesanta nove . . . ottanto!"*

She clapped and jumped by the red graffiti that was splashed by the fountain like the blood of a shattered kneecap in the news, the sketchpad stained with the fresh *mozzarella bufala* dripping from the fresh bread and chewed slowly with the sweet red pepper and the soft light on the orange stucco, the intense pleasure mixing with the loneliness until they seemed the same.

She became the city itself with its labyrinth of monuments and garbage in between, a woman hanging laundry by a temple and her bambino pissing on the broken stones.

She became the obscene halls of the Vatican with a great Angelico buried in a hidden chapel, everyone gathering with different noses and passports for *The Last Judgement* at the end of the winding stairs, Michelangelo's figures swirling up and down a wall the size of a basketball court and Christ like a referee in an almond of light.

Never before was art so beautiful as if the eyes were washed by the years of pain, the oculus in Hadrian's dome like a hole in the cranium to let the light through, the glow of selenite in San Giovanni so peaceful after a long day of walking alone, art as always a *"window into Eden." "Love genius,"* Blake said, *"it is the face of God,"* the paint that would fade from the wall that would crumble, Christ another bison in the limestone.

It was everywhere between her hills where the twins were suckled by the wolf and the altars once bloody with human sacrifice, the little city of art you could walk in a day with the Tiber at your side, a perfect place to start a civilization.

The Ancient City

In the middle of modern Rome at the other side of Michelangelo's *Campidoglio* on the Capitoline Hill there lies the huge void of *Il Foro*, the Forum of the original city once filled with temples and moneychangers. It is a monument now and you walk down the path as if into an abandoned quarry, our history in the few broken pieces of marble, the wisteria tumbling over the broken bricks.

See this space here, this chunk of marble leftover from the Huns, it was a temple of Venus before Caesar's time. And that broken column over there was another temple of another god or goddess now open to the clouds. Keep walking. For every space filled with rubble there was a temple and if you close your eyes you can still hear the moneychangers in the stalls.

One night while walking under a bright moon past the fence that surrounded it, no one inside but the cats and the ghosts, it was not the Forum anymore but felt like the abandoned lot by the perfume factory where we used to play after school and where one summer evening all the big kids gathered to watch the fight between Bonehead and Lefty.

"Zekey, you go home," Joey who lived across the street had said, "go on, gedada here, dis is fer big kids."

But Bonehead and Lefty were the two toughest kids in the neighborhood and their fight was too important to miss, Bonehead with his pockmarks and his crewcut and Lefty with his black silken hair and handsome face, Bonehead who was to become that unhappy cop who drank too much and Lefty that quiet man with a dry cleaning shop in Secaucus, their different lives locked for a moment like eternal forces. They seemed destined for that night and Lefty took out a pack of Chesterfields that was rolled in his shirtsleeves and handed it to one of his friends while Bonehead stood waiting and punching his palm. Then they circled each other and started swinging, Lefty hitting Bonehead in the face more than once and Bonehead wrestling him to the ground, broken glass everywhere and that they might be cut by it more scary than what they might do to each other. If Bonehead got the headlock it would be all over because though Lefty was the best boxer around Bonehead was as strong as a bulldog and would not let go. But then Lefty broke loose and started punching, both their faces bloody by now and the fight so bad that they could have killed each other if they had knives. But no one used knives in those days. To fight with the hands was the biggest part of growing up and though we might later become successful in business or profession the big fight was beneath them both and the way to manhood was the crouch and the fist.

Whether it was Bonehead or Lefty who won did not remain in memory, they had become so bloody that their friends may have broken them up, yet that night and their faces did not fade, and they and the abandoned lot became fused with the temples and Caesars a guide described to merchants on vacation, our race of warriors and our need to win and conquer, boys fighting while their mamas worked.

There seemed no end to it, our world of fighting and wanting more, the Sacred Wood of the Vestal Virgins littered with rusty cans, dozens of old condoms in the dirty yard of Santa Maria in Templo, the memory of you, Charlie, down by the Hudson when we were kids and you pointing to the green water. "Hey, Zekey, lookit dis scumbag ova here, it musta belonged to a camel."

No end to history, kids playing soccer in the Appian Way and tourists heading for the Colosseum.

"Ova here, Charlie, look, here's anudder one."

The white swirls of the Tiber flowed under the Ponte Cestio like Leonardo's beard. Study them, he seemed to whisper, follow the flowing water past the lovers under the arch, the tufts of green in the big white bricks and the long shadows of another sundown, keep making lines even of your own humpbacked shadow and the old fisherman's cap that Charlie found on the farm one afternoon and said, "Here, Zeke, here's a lucky cap for you to remember me with, you old bald bastard."

Your eyes are still vivid and the beauty mark still clear on your left
cheek, your sweeping hook shot on the side court where we had to
play when the big kids took over the good basket, your left-handed
penmanship and the curl of your fingers around those straight pens
that kept blotting your paper, your seat in the next row in back of the
room until Mrs. Flanagan put us on opposite sides where we made
faces behind her back, your voice that afternoon we sat on Mr.
Shwertheim's porch when it was raining and we watched the lightning and then counted until the thunder rumbled, you're here inside
this personal history that will end with these lines, this love flowing to
wherever it is they find a home.

Knucklebones and Yoghurt

· Did I tell you what happened to my nose?
· Oh you and your nose again.
· I had cancer on it from too much sun.
· Don't go to a doctor, he'll cut it off.
· I did go to a doctor. I'm not afraid of doctors. I went and sat in his
  office for over an hour and then the nurse put me in one of those
  closets and I had to sit there for almost another hour.
· They treat us like chickens.
· You went to a rich doctor. You should have gone to a poor doctor.
· There are no more poor doctors.
· Knucklebones was a poor doctor.
· That's because he didn't have a license.
· No one went to him because his hands used to shake.
· I went to him once when I cut my arm. Everyone said, "Weren't you
  afraid?" But I tell you he sewed my arm perfect and for how much?
  For two dollars as if he was a shoemaker.
· They're all shoemakers. You think they know what they're doing?
· They saved my life.
· What about your nose?
· I don't know yet about my nose. It's okay now, I keep it shaded by
  wearing my grandson's baseball hat when I work in the garden. The
  doctor gave me some ointment to put on my face but the next day my
  face was like a strawberry, there were sores all over.
· It was the wrong medicine.

- They have so many medicines they don't know the difference anymore.
- I threw it in the garbage and put yoghurt on my face instead.
- I was just going to tell you that. I used to put yoghurt on my son's back everytime he'd get sunburned at the beach.
- I put it on and it made the old skin peel off and now my face is normal.
- Did you tell the doctor?
- I never went back. The nurse called me for a checkup but I said no thanks.
- They just want more money.
- Sometimes you just have to say shit to doctors.
- Sometimes you have to cure yourself.
- If you have the will, some people don't have the will.
- You can have all the will you want. Your nose is one thing, your life is another. Anoosh Toomah had all the will in the world and I saw her waste away like the roses that I prune.

She Doesn't Live In A Temple Anymore

On the way to Athens the young people slept in the seats of the lounge and while the ship plowed through the early morning darkness the island of Ithaca lay a few miles to starboard. From the deck in the slashing wind the waves seemed merciless and the ghost of a middle-aged Odysseus held tight to a timber. Would he make it? Would the beautiful Nausicca revive him and the kind Phaecians carry him home? He held on while the dark waves devoured his friends and the young squeezed together in their fetal curls.

They were like ourselves at that age and our hunger for other shores, our dysentery in dark hotels and our bags by the road, Tony shivering in a doorway in Paris on Christmas eve and Leo sick in Tehran, Shlomo on a freighter to Holland and Dolores in Spain with a suitcase of diapers. We survived, we made it this far, only a little more to go before the trip is over.

Athens was full of smog and traffic and the only reason for staying was to see the Parthenon.

It was out of view behind a military wall and the long path climbed through a tourist village, yet despite the smog that shrouded the city

below the weather was gorgeous and the morning had been very pleasant with buns and coffee in the Plaka. The clouds curled like gods
above the hill while the ghosts of slaves struggled with oxen to pull the
marble up the trail.

Then came the rubble. More rubble and the great white columns
rising into the blue with nothing inside them but rubble.

It was more than just immense, its size intensified by the open
space. Yet all that stuff in the art books about proportion and line was
really true, the magical lines made it feel as natural and friendly as a
grove of redwoods and a place not of mystery but an everyday wonder
anyone could have.

It was still a wonder, though most of it was gone. It was like an old
woman with her tits gone and the color gone from her hair and only
her smile left to let you guess the beauty of her youth.

It was still alive. The roof was gone, the paint was gone and there
were only the columns left like a cadaver with a smile, a pickled hunk
of meat in a medical school for students too young to see that the flesh
they were slicing had never died, that the wonder of its form was still
alive as they traced the intricate nerves and tried to hide their horror
with jokes.

How it must have glowed in the wilderness, the temple of Athena
who was born from a forehead by the hammer of art, her crippled
brother bursting her free from the thunder and lightning.

She was not there anymore, the great chryselephantine figure that
once stood in the cella at a height too colossal to imagine was now who
knew where in ivory knick-knacks and gold fillings, Phidias rotting in
prison and Socrates dead by poison. And the great sculptures, well
you know what happened to them, the great heads and torsos lying
scattered among dying Turks when the Venetians tested their new
cannon, art and life one at last and the marble carried back down the
hill by the progeny of slaves who used it for butcher blocks.

A few pieces remained, a few pathetic pieces in a huge gallery in the
British Museum, a broken torso, a head of a horse, a broken-faced god
without hands or feet and the rainy afternoons a young art student
never failed to visit them.

He used to go after class every Tuesday and Thursday, and the broken-
faced god would always be there with his knee up and his arms open
as if he were neither indifferent nor concerned but rapt inside the

marble with the spirit of Phidias somewhere inside his magical pose.

What made him so beautiful, what was his secret?

Over and over the young student copied him and each time came to the void where the hands should have been, a vision of death he once tried to fill by drawing those hands and they turned out like links of sausage dangling in Gagliardi's butcher shop.

What a beautiful young art student he was, he was as beautiful as the god he could not imitate and yet he hated himself and wanted to die. Why don't I just kill myself, he thought, when no matter how hard I try I'll never make anything beautiful? And yet why did he even

want to make something beautiful if it did not reflect someone inside him?

Someone was locked inside him and he struggled to burst her free. He copied and copied as if he were hammering at a forehead and as if the nervous breakdowns he was heading for would crack his shell.

The first one came when Nelly went away. He broke into pieces and they lay scattered like all the sketches he would throw in the garbage. He didn't want to go near the museum, the very thought of beauty made him nauseous. The weeks passed with crying and sleeping until he could slowly stop smoking and breathe again. Then one sunny afternoon on one of those balmy days around Whitsuntide when everyone was outside enjoying the end of the rains he found himself walking around Bloomsbury near the museum and he stopped to eat a sandwich in the little park nearby. He threw crumbs to the sparrows and watched the people and the closer he looked the more beautiful they became, everywhere was so beautiful with the pulse of life inside all the people and the sparrows and the plane trees and he realized that the pulse was in himself as well and suddenly he thought of the broken pieces of marble inside the museum and he felt no, they don't belong in that room, they belong in the sunshine on a temple where everyone could sit nearby and feed the sparrows. What was it like, he wondered, that original temple where they came from? He had always wanted to see it.

Turkish Songs and Armenian Moslems

· I saw Satenig last week. She just came back from Russia.
· It's not Russia. It's Armenia.
· It's still Russia.
· But we have our language there. All the street signs are in Armenian.
· They may use our language but I can hardly understand them when they speak.
· Half of their words are Russian.
· It's still our language.
· People make too much of language.
· To tell you the truth, I enjoy speaking Turkish more. It was my first tongue.

· Some of us hate it. The Dashnaks even want to change the words in the songs.

· They can't change the words. All the pleasure is in the words.

· No, they say, the words are filth.

· Listen, I know what filth is.

· I know you know.

· They lay on top of me and they left me for dead. Every one of them lay on top of me and I was only fourteen and I will never stop hating them. But when I hear their songs I love their strings and their words.

· You can say that.

· I can say it.

· Because she loves music.

· It isn't only their music. It's our music too.

· They invited my uncle to play for them. My uncle Vosdanig played the zither and my uncle Mateos sang. My uncle Mateos had the best voice in the whole city and sang for the Pasha himself, but when the massacre started his head was cut off.

· It's our music more than their music.

· It's our land too.

· It's no one's land if no one lives on it.

· No one wants to live there.

· Everyone wants to live here.

· There are still some of us left back there.

· Those who are left are Moslems.

· So even if they are Moslems, they're still Armenians.

· How can an Armenian be a Moslem?

· Nubar's sister is a Moslem now, if she's still alive. After her husband was killed a Moslem took her for his wife. She had four children with him. Nubar went back and wanted her to leave, but no, she said, how could she leave her children? Her children are Moslems now but they're still Nubar's nieces and nephews.

· Isn't that something, Nubar who was such a passionate Dashnak?

· He hardly knows the difference anymore. All he does is sit on the porch and tell his childhood stories.

She Begins To Reveal Herself In Fairyland

At the border the Turkish guards searched the bus and there was a long wait by the river, the lush green of the other shore filled with poppies and lupine. Come, it seemed to say, come through the gate of flowers and bones.

It opened into a landscape like a dream, the same glow of soft sienna and new spring grass, the boys on the buses sprinkling lemon cologne in everyone's palm and the faces everywhere seeming to smell as fragrant. Were these the faces that raped Aunty Zabel, were these the eyes that slaughtered Uncle Avedis?

They stared back like innocent models. Nowhere else, not even in India, were they more friendly and hospitable. They heard of the past but it was not theirs, it was erased from their history books.

Should they have owned it, should they have paid for it? They sat like Harlem and Benares in homemade scarves and brightly colored caps, the empire of the Golden Bough reduced to unemployment and Saint Sophia gutted and crumbling, the great mosaics another page in a guidebook.

Yet the land was rich with abundant streams and the road unravelled into a wild interior like Wyoming before the white man. Kayseri was the frontier town at the edge of the wilderness and from there on the bus was empty. It climbed the snow-ribbed mountains as if departing from civilization, the chubby gold-toothed driver tapping his steering wheel in rhythm to the vibrant music on the scratchy radio, the ancient sas and zither twanging into the new green cottonwoods and exotic storks, the mud homes nestled in the high rocks like pueblo adobes.

Suddenly in the middle of nowhere the bus stopped and the only other passenger got off.

Where was he going, his plastic slippers trodding in the snow in the middle of nowhere?

He disappeared as if into fairyland.

As if into Uncle Jacko and Mano who used to play backgammon in Mano's little grocery shop in Weehawken, nothing to do but sit on the barrel of olives and watch them slap the board and roll the dice with their hearty *yalahs*.

As if into Aunty Shooshanig who had a cross tatooed on her hand when she was a girl in Jerusalem and so she was called *Haji* Shoosho like all other oriental Christians who visited the holy sepulchre.

As if into Aunty Lucinah who had that wooden camel from Alexandria where she lived before she could come to America.

As if into all those who were left behind. All those who were driven through these beautiful mountains with the weak ones slipping or jumping to their deaths, their screams echoing in a passionate love-song from the nearest radio station, the jolly driver tapping in tune with the exciting lament and the twang of the sas waving through the air like a suicide falling to the rocks below.

The bus continued and the voyage unfurled to quiet villages and delicious food, the cities crowded with the unemployed and kids carrying NATO rifles. In Malatya there was a *dolmush* to a town in the high country called Arapkir. There was supposed to be some Armenians around there.

It was a small town like Tombstone in *My Darling Clementine* and the locals gathered around a Marco Polo and watched him struggle with his pocket dictionary. Hey guys, look what we got here, a real live one.

The dictionary was useless and the only word that worked was the one they never heard anymore.

"*Ermeni.*" Armenian.

Ermeni! *Ermeni*! Oh sure, we know what that is! And they commanded a boy to run down the road and then babbled on as if the dictionary could translate.

The boy returned with an ancient woman wearing slippers and pajamas.

She came closer with her big nose and wild eyebrows, the raspy words tumbling from her lower lip and suddenly exploding the days of no one to talk with. She almost whispered them.

"*Hye-es?*" Are you Armenian?

The two syllables slipped between her few teeth like a welcome mat to love and death. Was there any way to say no?

No to Armenian? No to history and vengeance? No to big noses and paklava? No to identity and death?

"*Io. Hye-em*" Yes, I'm Armenian.

Yes Armenian and not donkey, yes the strange face in the mirror while the others sat and listened, the foreign tongue once purged

from their mountains now returning in a bald American with a down vest, the words they never heard from the shopkeeper who as a child was rescued by one of them and who became one of them and who was now incomprehensible.

"Look, a glass of *chay*, the owner of the cafe honors you."

"He honors me?"

"Of course, you are a stranger. He must offer you hospitality."

They stared at the down vest and wanted to know how much it cost.

"I should buy them *chay*."

"No, that would be an insult. Drink it and let's go to my shop."

She led the way down a dirt road to an open stall the size of three large canvasses, the mud walls covered with shelves of soap and buttons.

It was not just a stall, it was like a cave somewhere in prehistory, an orgone box two little boys once built on a sidewalk with those big pieces of cardboard from Schwarzenbach's factory, the grown-ups walking by and the warm darkness vibrating inside.

Her Armenian name was Nevart, Nevart Hairabedian. She said it with a nod as if it belonged to an old friend she hadn't seen in eighty years.

And with her lips as the words flowed through them, with her big and spotted nose like the nose of old Oghidah the little seamstress on Sixteenth Street who was Bobby Sahagian's grandmother and the aunt of Annie Ohannesian who married Haig Pinajian, the yoghurt man, the woof of genes and language seemed to cross the time zones and weave into the warp of a personal history with yet another pattern, old Oghidah sitting by the window with the door open in the summertime and nodding for two little boys to come in and have a cold glass of *Seven-Up* from her wooden ice-box, Charlie the non-Armenian sharing it just as he shared the sweets from his grandfather who smoked guinea rolls and played bocceball in the alley, Charlie who was Italian and whose mother served anise biscuits with milk in her kitchen after school, Charlie who when he wanted to be mean could say, "Joe DiMaggio, Phil Rizzuto, Sal Maglio, and dare aint even one Armeeny-yin inna whole majer leagues."

She had married a Turk and her children and grandchildren were now in Istanbul, but she preferred to stay in the back country. She had relatives in Philadelphia, her father's sister's children, but they didn't want anything to do with Turks.

"They would spit at me."

She stood at the edge of town and pointed to the river below. There were some other Armenians across the valley. There was a bridge to cross and the village would be in the rocks. She gave directions with her fingers in the air like a magus with a dove.

The Ghosts

· I wish I could write. I make marks on paper to help me remember and then I forget what they're for.

· That's okay, just keep trying. Don't lose your memory. If our memories go we're finished.

· I forget everything now. I can't remember yesterday and sixty years ago seems like this morning.

· Call me up and I'll tell you the difference. You remind me and I'll remind you.

· We have to keep remembering or we'll be like Zarzavart in the nursing home. If you go there now she won't even know who you are.

· She doesn't want to know who I am. I never really liked her to tell you the truth.

· She lost touch with her family, that's how she got like that. There was no one to talk with but the walls.

· There's always someone to talk with. You can talk with the plants, you can talk with the cat, you can talk with the old Chinese man around the corner who's half deaf and can't understand anything you say but at least he pretends to. Zarzavart didn't want to talk with just anyone, she was always too private.

· She talks with ghosts now. She looks out the window and talks with the ghosts in her head.

She Doesn't Leave Anyone Alone

The river was the Euphrates and the letters curved on the map like a name we all had in common. At the bridge there was a sweet spot by some cottonwoods and the river was cold and swift like those in the Sierras, but so far it was still unpolluted and tasted delicious.

The village appeared about an hour later and was almost hidden in the huge rocks that towered above like monuments to oblivion.

Once Armenian, once Persian, once Mede or Hittite or the nameless stone age tribe whose tombs became the fields of wheat, it now belonged to yet another ring of genes that settled in the homes of those who died in the desert.

There was a fountain in the center and the stones caught the swift stream and bent it into a mini-waterfall where the veiled women giggled in their palms when the stranger tried to wash his underwear and socks.

When Boghos heard of it he shook his head and sucked his palette.

"Tzt. It is shameful for a man to do that, it is woman's work."

He rolled another cigarette with his cheap government tobacco and sat against the wall of the mud home he built with his hands and nothing else, the frame from young poplar trees and the wall textured with the sweeps of his trowel, the soft white color from the special mud he had to cart from the other side of the ridge.

Gambar, his Moslem neighbor, helped him. Gambar also rolled a cigarette and offered it to the *musafer*, the guest, whose name he got a big kick out of yelling all the time, the only word he could communicate with.

"Zay-kay! Zay-kay!"

He looked more Armenian than Boghos, the two of them as close as birch trees with a common root, the both born during the massacre and reunited after forty years when Boghos returned from a factory in Istanbul where his mother had escaped.

Another story, another knot in the tapestry of everyone killed or gone to Fresno or Shanghai, the great scythe scattering big noses across the continents. They were back together again as in the dream of Charlie coming back, Boghos translating and asking what life was like in America.

"Hos laveh yevsa hone?" Is it better here or there?

There was no answer in the swoon of their simple life, the days passing with pleasant shits in the cool clean stall next to the cow manger and the tin can of water for washing the asshole, the air clean and full of chickens gurgling and cows mooing, the butter churning in the swooshing goatskin and the flatbread puffing on the stove, Manooshag rolling the dough and punching it like a pizza, Gambar's grandkids peeking at the stranger with the sketchpad.

Boghos crunched a juicy scallion and winked as he sucked his side teeth.

"*Kefeh hos, kef.*" Kef, it is here.

Kef like a mantra in the rhythm of his life, to taste it and enjoy it and make more of it, the overflowing gourd and the sigh of a quiet belly, his eyes closed to its vibrant pulse, the untranslatable *kef* that was born and raised in this land like a giant watermelon bursting with sweetness, all was *kef* at the end of suffering. He pursed and nodded in agreement with himself, Boghos who survived because his father became a Moslem, Boghos who saved his lira to return to his childhood and was now less anything than the same creased and stubbled face in the same sienna tan of the same earth he shared with Gambar who was less Moslem than a big smile and brown teeth, both of them holding on to their cows and their wheat in their seasons.

He rubbed mint in his palms and held it to his nostrils. The goats nayed in the distance and the cock followed with his sprung rhythm, the cow mooed like an echo from the bowels of the earth and from the field came the bray of the donkey all by himself, the haws rising up the hill as if from the bones in the desert with a gripping lament and flowing praise.

In the spare room up the ladder the darkness and silence were so deep they felt like things in themselves, the heavy quilts redolent of childhood.

Stay here, they beckoned, don't go on. Why go on when there's only history to repeat, stay till the money runs out and then catch a disease and die. Die in the blackness, don't wake up to the same old Zeke.

But in the rest from the weariness of travelling the dreams were strong and just before dawn a powerful erection reached out and a beautiful woman stared at it.

"*That's a good key you have there,*" she said, and she opened her legs and fucked while standing, the waves surging and flowering be-

hind the eyes at the moment of waking, the semen wiped on the pajamas before it dripped on the clean sheet.

The cock crowed and forms appeared again. Another morning alive, more lines, Through the tiny window the dawn was red and blue and in the glow between the mountains the morning star, Venus, floated inside the cradle of an infant moon like the Moslem symbol so hated by those who use the cross. She was gone but she would come back again, she wouldn't leave anyone alone.

The Wound

It was on the morning of the dream that the wound occurred. The once a week mail van was to stop by the village and take on anyone who wanted to go to Kharpet, the next city. Manooshag had prepared a lunch of soft cheese wrapped in sheets of bread she baked the night before. She stuffed it in the bag with the dried mulberries and the pumpkin seeds and Boghos waved for the guest to join him on the rug. The hot *chay* steaming from the brass pot and the fresh butter and quince jelly were like a Chardin on the breakfast sheet and the room was bathed with the colored shadows of the early light. Then suddenly the peaceful silence ripped apart with a blinding flash, the guest unaware that the *chay* was moved and his foot scalded when he kicked it over, Manooshag rushing in with some blue liquid but the skin was already peeling.

Don't go, they said, stay until it heels. But he ignored it and didn't want to miss the van.

Manooshag stood by the door when she said goodbye, her long underwear beneath her pajamas and her ruddy face like someone in Millet or *Barney Google and Snuffy Smith*.

Gambar joined Boghos on the path to the road and he waved his hand in the Asian gesture of fondness and sadness combined.

Waiting by the road their faces gleamed in the long rays as if the sun were an acid and the love for them a burin, their lives etched in memory with the towering rocks, their tobacco teeth and stubbled faces fusing with the earth they plowed. Their big mustaches were like wings for their smiles and the burn on the foot like a souvenir that they were not a dream.

Gambar the Moslem babbled something eagerly for Boghos to translate.

"*Geseh yegur noren. Amaren yegur, chooreh ger tank, dsug udenk.*" He says come again. Come in the summertime and we'll go down to the river and eat fish.

She Stares Across the Cobbles

The foot got worse while the Euphrates disappeared and her twin, the Tigris, led the way to the ancient city of Diyarbkekir, her walls of black stone like a huge castle on the mesa above the plains.

In what had been the Armenian quarter, once the richest part of town, the bucolic sheperdess of the high country had become a tabid Kurdish girl who sold herself in a filthy lane, her gaunt face flashing back to a ghetto long ago.

She stood on the other side of the cobbles as if in a double vision of past and present, her sad eyes exposed with the old photographs of a dead father. This was the ancient city where he was born, that little boy who posed with his pointy slippers and baggy pants, his big mustached brothers beside him like mythical cowboys and his long-haired sister holding his hand like a darling Clementine.

Was it in this house or that one, the little whore staring back at a crippled stranger as he tried to focus between his romance and her misery?

These were the donkey lanes where his father played stickball with his gang, all those kids like little Carnig whose son became a commissioner in Weehawken and little Miran whose son became a billionaire on Long Island and little Yerem who made a fortune with hotdogs, each of them now Republican and retired in Palm Springs or Florida.

These were the homes of Sunday feasts and evenings filled with music, Uncle Avedis playing the zither and Uncle Ashod singing like waves of wild wheat.

These were the doorways of all those who did not escape, their bones the sand in the Tigris below.

"*Your uncles were taken across the bridge and killed by sword.*" But what did it mean, "*killed by sword,*" the image in a nephew's mind like a scene in a film where the camera turns away? How could he paint the sharp steel slicing through their flesh and their heads dropping in the sand like those in El Salvador or Cambodia?

She stared across the cobbles as if she were the ghost of aunt Armen who was drowned with her long red hair floating in the bloody waves. She was the vision that couldn't be focused in the blur of beauty and horror, all the beautiful and miserable creatures in the images and songs that win fame for artists.

Some ragged kids surrounded the pilgrim and wanted his pen. *"Turisti, turisti!"*

The foot oozed and swelled like a slimy vegetable, the pain tempering the excitement on the long walks through the slums of history.

From Diyarbekir the journey would continue through more hometowns and the never-ending saga of mythical kin.

Through Severek where Harry Goshgarian's aunt was beheaded and through Urfa where Charlie Aramian's grandfather was tortured and hung by his feet.

Through Gazantap where Willy Mazoujian's mother starved to death and through Bireçik where Kerop Bedoukian survived on a handful of raisins a day and through Osmaniye where Jack Chorbajian's uncle became a slave and later escaped to Bulgaria, each day the foot getting worse and the pain seeming to throb in rhythm with the long-haired goats of a rolling landscape and the flowing zither on a bus driver's radio, the terror of history impossible to draw, all drawing a transformation and every suffering doomed to become art.

Flesheaters

· There's no taste in meat anymore.

· Not to young people. They love it, they eat it twice a day.

· Every once in a while I have a craving for a piece of steak, but it doesn't taste like what I wanted.

· What kind of steak you eat? I eat the senior citizen special and it tastes delicious.

· I'm going to eat cheese. They're giving cheese away downtown.

· I went down there. There was a line two blocks long and the old people were fainting on the sidewalk from waiting so long.

· Nevertheless I see people in Cadillacs coming to get it.

· I miss the cheese we use to get from the Dough-eaters.

- The Dough-eaters here don't make it, they buy their mozzarella in the supermarket.
- I had a lot of friends who were Dough-eaters.
- They're Christians. They drink the wine and eat the wafer.
- I had friends who were Jewish too.
- They have their own wine and wafer.
- It's all the same grapes and the same wheat.

She Offers Herself To Be Killed And Eaten

"When you get to Adana, my son, look for the river and the bridge. Our acre was on the other side of the river and we crossed the bridge to get there."

There was a new bridge for the highway but the old one was still used for carts and bicycles. The weather was gorgeous and the park by the river was filled with a promenade of families on their Sunday in the open, the Mediterranean softness the same as when St. Paul was here or when Anthony met Cleopatra, the sky cerulean and the river reflecting it, swirling in spate from the snowy Taurus to its mouth at Mersin, swift and whitecapped under the Roman arches.

There was no point in going to the other side, especially by foot. The bus passed through on the way to the station, the acre now a suburb of tickytacks and the little shack a gasoline pump, the grapes a *Coca-Cola* sign and the donkey making way for U.S. Army trucks.

There was no point in anything, every point became a line and every line led to another. There was nothing and yet it moved, a line reaching into the void like a boy fishing on a bridge.

Who was that little boy? Was his great-grandfather a rapist, did his great-grandmother swing a hatchet?

He was the ghost of uncle Arshag. He was the boy in love with light, his pencil and his love of drawing now a fishing pole and a line swaying in the flickering coins on the windswept waves, his black hair shining in the long spokes of the floating sun.

He waited. He waited with the young patience that was the seed of faith and courage, his pole pointing up and his line reaching into the deep.

The fish would bite. If not now then soon and if not soon then so what, he was a fisherman and his float bobbed on the waves like his heart. He reeled it in and reached again for the flashing prize that would leap from the waves like his soul. He would touch it delicately and hold his breath as he slipped the hook from its innocent lips and then he would slide it in the pail where it would somehow live and die at the same time, its eyes open as it suffocated, his own special life whose head he would slice on a chunk of marble and whose blood would glue his fingers, his flesh to eat until his own be eaten in turn.

He waited with his face glowing in the dying light, the moon rising and the red horizon bleeding into purples and blues.

He would be wounded. He would catch his fish but he would become a cripple and for the rest of his life he would suffer as he struggled to be whole again. He would lose the fish in the river and he would keep casting his line to catch it again.

Would the casting make him whole, would each line help him?

Night came and the guide in the stomach led the way to a fragrant restaurant in a labyrinth of quiet lanes.

There was no fish, there was only shish-kebab and the memories wafting from its aroma.

The barbecues one lucky summer when Mama made enough money to go to Belmar and the meat tasting delicious in Vahan's backyard.

The slaughtered lamb that hung in the butcher's window and the blue eyes always open, the smack of Gagliardi's heavy knife through the leg bones and the shoulder bones and his cold bloody hands twisting the shiny balls and sockets.

The knucklebones Mama used to dry and then throw on the rug to show how children played with them in the old country.

The lamb on the farm in Freehold and the thick oilyness of its wool, the big eyes staring back like the vault of the universe.

The odor of the slaughterhouse in Newark and the slice in Gagliardi's finger when his knife slipped.

The wood of the barbecue becoming charcoal and the taste of blood and ash.

A young handsome waiter served it with juicy tomatoes and a slightly burnt pepper. The fresh bread sopped the bloody juice and the hungry pilgrim stuffed it in his mouth with a memory of a friend's farm in Montana and a rabbit who had to be killed for an evening meal.

He had cuddled her in his arm and petted her behind her ear not only to calm her down but to love her. He loved her, he loved that rabbit.

But there was no room to be squeamish, if the club missed she would suffer even more and he hit her perfectly between her frightened stare and her twitching nose.

He held her like an only child and rubbed her hind paws as if they were his own. He felt for the space between the tendon and the bone and following Max's directions he pierced the skin with the big rusty nails on the barn wall and let her hang head down, feeling and yet not feeling the sharp points pierce her skin as if it were a membrane between the worlds.

She hung with her legs open and there was no stopping, even if he pulled her free her brain was crushed. And yet she was still alive and pulling her head to stretch her neck he sliced it off as quickly as he could as if her freedom depended on his speed.

He shouldn't have. He should have cut it slowly and felt for the main arteries and nerves that were the channels of the life she shared with him, the knife an extension of his hand and a memory that should never fade so that every time he ate a rabbit or a kernal he would feel a life dying to feed his own.

He dropped her head in the bucket and yet though headless she was not a "carcass" or a hunk of "meat" but was still a rabbit and now even more so as if her death had revealed her essence. He cut away her tail and her front feet and then her skin around her hind paws and then loosening her skin around her rump and being careful to leave her fat on her flanks he peeled her skin off and now she was even less a "carcass" or a package in a supermarket, her naked flesh like his own and with the same beauty he had studied for so long and he began butchering her with all his talent for drawing the nude.

He cut through her pelvic bone and sliced a straight line from her vulva to the void of her head and her viscera spilled open as if in birth, her entrails and organs not only like his own but life itself, the coils and fibers like the universe in miniature, the red, blue and yellow swirl of the galaxies and the dying suns. As delicately as if he were drawing nipples or hairs he cut away her urine sac and then scooped her guts and dropped them in the bucket for her cousin the pig who still had a year to live.

"Good job," Max said, "you have a talent for this."

Max was a dear friend and that night he shared his home and his

*candles and Judith cooked the rabbit with rosemary and garlic, the
pieces chewed slowly as if death could be tasted but all that came was
the warmth and thankfulness of sharing a meal with loved ones.*

She was not dead. She was the eternal rabbit who fed the love of
friends and was tortured in cages with her eyes pinned open and a
researcher burning them with experimental mascaras.

She would never die, she would continue to be slaughtered in the
name of yet another religion called science and a young student would
cut her apart to earn a degree.

She would go on feeding a hungry artist who could never taste her
death.

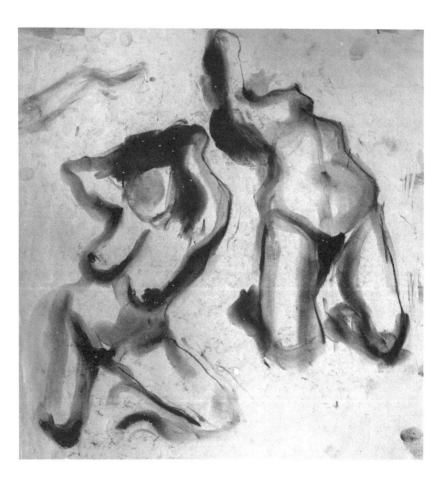

He left a tip for the waiter and walked outside. The neighborhood was dark and the women had disappeared from the streets, the men drifting to different cafes to watch television and play backgammon.

The night was warm and a full moon followed a limping shadow along the river, its glow reflected in the waves and its silver train like a carpet for his foot, his belly full and his head floating from the two glasses of arak, the taste of lamb and coriander still in his mouth.

The Butt of The Navel and The Circumcision

· I remember when you were a girl. When I look at you I remember you then.
· So what?
· The more some people remember the more they hate.
· There are brothers and sisters who can't stand to be in the same room.
· Not only brothers and sisters. There are daughters and sons who don't want to see their mothers. Can you imagine that, children who don't love their mother?
· Who knows, maybe if I knew my mother I wouldn't love her either. Maybe she was a pinch of the nose just like me.
· You have to love your mother. Even if you don't want to, you have to.
· Shoeshine Leo didn't have to. He put her in Florida and never saw her again.
· That's because she ruined his life. He was in love with a Dough-eater and she made such a stink the girl ran away.
· So what? He married a good Armenian girl and had full-blooded Armenian children. She was right to make a stink.
· I would never do that with my daughter. I don't care who she marries.
· If your daughter marries this world will be heaven.
· She moves around too much.
· I know, it's because the butt of her navel was not buried. My oldest girl was born at home and after the cord was tied the old women buried the butt of her navel in the yard. But my youngest was born in the hospital and who knows what they did with the butt of her navel?
· She's still out there looking for it.
· Don't worry, she'll get married.

- People don't get married anymore, it costs too much to get divorced.
- Girls here don't know how to grab a husband, that's what Charcoal Oghidah used to say. "I was the ugliest girl in Diyarbekir," she used to say, "but that didn't stop me. There was a boy I liked so I made my father get him drunk and then I slept with him and that was that. I was ugly but I gave him four beautiful children and don't you worry, he came to love me too."
- A girl can't do that anymore, it doesn't work.
- It works on my television story.
- No it won't. Scott is not going to marry Sue-Ellen just because she's going to have a baby.
- Poor girl.
- There are lots of them out there, all those girls who are alone.
- They're like orphans.
- When I was in the orphanage we all wanted to get married so we could leave, and yet we hardly knew what a boy was made of.
- There was a boy in my orphanage who just missed being slaughtered. He was about eleven years old and they circumcized him to make him a Moslem. I thought it meant they made him a eunuch. Everyone said it was very painful for him. He also had a good voice and they made him learn their prayers. Every morning and evening he would climb the minaret and sing their prayers and I used to think he was crying for the loss of his balls.

She Washes Her Cunt and Then Wipes It Clean

From Adana the bus climbed the Taurus Mountains and crossed the yellow dervish plains to Ankara. In a hotel in Ankara there was a doctor from Pakistan on an exchange program for Third World countries and he said that if there was no fever the foot was probably not infected but it should be kept clean and rested.

Back in Istanbul it began to heal and the raw flesh slowly formed a scab. After a week of lying by a window the swelling was gone and the cripple could walk again. Every day he watched the different colors of the wound become brown and crusted as if with varnish and the healing seemed like a miracle. The joy of walking without pain seemed like a miracle and he went outside as if reborn. What foolishness it was, he felt, to want anything but to witness the miracle of life. And yet what was life but living and he wanted more of it.

He went outside and joined the faces that flowed between the continents, the bridge across the Bosporus full of little fish restaurants and the little pretzel monger selling huge pretzels that were a meal in themselves, the cucumber man peeling and salting fresh cucumbers for only about ten cents each. The colorful boats bobbed in the gentle current as if they were alive and the Golden Horn bathed in a renaissance light, the phallic minarets and the vulva dome of a mosque pulsing in its glow. Everywhere seemed pulsing with the miracle of life and a horny convalescent wanted to fuck every part of it, a bewildered taxi driver looking over his shoulder as he tried to pronounce the words in his little dictionary.

"*Orospu? Fahishe?* Prosteetoot?"

The driver curved through a labyrinth and arrived near some soldiers checking identifications in a narrow lane. He nodded and pointed at a row of shops down the lane and a crowd of men gathered around each of them.

They were not shops. There was no glass in the windows and the women inside were like naked mannequins come to life, the fantasy of women everywhere unclothed was suddenly real and each one was a version of the miracle of life.

She stood in the back and filed her nails.

She sat up front and cupped her tits in her palms.

She crouched with her buttocks raised and pointed at her bush.

She hissed and twirled her tongue.

Come, she hissed, come buy the darkness of my bush.

The men stared like children without money in a candystore and one of them brayed and shuddered as if he would come every day and make up for all the years of jerking off. He would make up for a life devoted to lines that earned no money and all the women who said no because of money. He would make up for the world of money and the kind of suffering that went with it.

Here now was the money for the woman of the underworld, his emigrant money coming back to the land of bones. He could finally pay for her who disappeared so long ago.

But which one was she and yet what difference did it make? Why the hesitation as in the recurring dream of a bakery and a boy unable to choose between the different loaves, each one baked with the same

dough and yet he couldn't choose, time was running out and he couldn't choose, he couldn't choose.

She could not be chosen. She came and went like the weather and all he could do was enjoy her or resist. She was like a night many years ago when he was driving a cab on an evening shift and came back to his commune exhausted and in deep despair. She was the grace who dissolved that despair.

It had been raining all night but stopped when he got back in the early morning. He had stood in the soft drizzle that glimmered in the street-light on the corner and he didn't want to go inside. He didn't want to go back to his life, he wanted to die with the drizzle washing his face and making him clean again. But he didn't die, he was tired and hungry and when he went inside Mary was still up and she was sit-ting by the kitchen.

She had been visiting the commune and was staying only until she got herself together to continue south. She was always playing loud rock music and cooking exotic meals that weren't worth her pile of dishes and her mess. She would always be sitting around and laugh-ing and chatting while a miserable artist was unable to paint. He tried to ignore her and sometimes even insulted her but she didn't seem to mind as if somewhere inside her she knew he would love her someday. He didn't know anything about her or want to know and she liked it like this. She had a kind of shyness that was the other side of snobbery and she liked to keep an air of mystery around her even though she was never any good at it. She would do things like take her clothes out of the dryer and put a stylish dress on and walk around like Greta Garbo except for the nylon panties stuck on her buttocks from the static. She had a kind of awkwardness he secretly loved and yet he ignored her because she didn't look right, her hips were too large and her face too wide and he was too busy thinking about someone else.

She was quiet that night and everyone else was asleep except for the fish swimming back and forth in the rainbow lights of the big green tank. She was sitting on the other side of the room as the weary hack plopped in the sofa and moaned about not eating anything all day and being too exhausted to get up and fix a sandwich.

"Would you like me to fix you a sandwich?" she asked. "Mary," he said, "if you fixed me a sandwich I would appreciate it more than

anything else in the world and I don't care if it's one of your concoctions or not."

She made it as if it were her masterpiece, the picture or song inside her she wanted to give to the world and at this moment especially to him because she liked him, she thought he was weird, he was like a child even though he was much older than she and his craziness was very interesting.

He lay on the sofa with a good feeling that can come with weariness and he didn't have to do anything but just sit there and be served. She sat across the room and watched the hungry man eat her sandwich and chew it slowly with gratitude. How delicious it was, he told her, and she seemed to be able to taste it through him. Then when he was finished she listened to him moan about his back again.

"Would you like a massage?" she asked. "Mary," he said, "if you gave me a massage now I would appreciate it more than anything else in the world." "Would you?" she said. "Yes, I would," he said, and she asked him to undress and he didn't care if she thought he was too skinny or whatever, he didn't care what she thought of him and with his eyes buried in his arm he felt her hand go down his spine and give him an erection.

"Mary, you got the sweetest hands I ever felt." "Oh comon." "No, really." "Just be quiet and relax." "Mary, you've given me an erection." "Have I? How nice." "Mary, would you like a massage, too?" "I would if you'd like to."

The touch of her flesh was like a glow he could embrace and the body he had ignored for so long was like food to his starving hands and lips.

"Wait," she said, "lie on your back for me," and for the first time in his life he felt he didn't have to do anything to get what he needed, he didn't have to stay hard and fuck whoever she was for as long as she needed to come, all he had to do was lie back and let her suck him and take her time and when she had enough he wanted to lick her too, her cunt was as lovely as her face and kissing it he could feel her streaming and he slipped inside her and fucked her with the waves flowing between them.

"Mary," he whispered, "you're beautiful." "Oh comon," she said and yet somewhere inside her she believed him and she smiled with love for herself through his love for her. "Yes," you are, he said, and if his life had been spent in one massive wave of selfishness he felt he

could die knowing that at least for one moment he had helped a young woman realize how beautiful she was, Mary who had such a distorted view of herself and was always thinking there was something wrong with her. She curled into him under his old musty sleeping bag in the attic with the candle flinging shadows across the beams and falling asleep in the fragrance of her hair he looked forward to being with her again and again.

But she was gone the next day. It was her last night there and she hadn't told him. She had slipped out of bed very quietly and left a note on his sketchpad. "Dear Zeke, thank you for last night. I believed you when you said you loved me. I love you too. Sincerely, Mary."

She wanted to travel. She had been in Tacoma, Washington all her life and she wanted to see the rest of the world before she settled down and had kids. She would have two of them before he would hear of her again and her husband would be a big guy who planted trees and she would live in Oregon and struggle to stay out of the city.

He would never forget her though her face would fade. He would remember her without a face in different cities around the world and he would keep hoping to find again the grace of her tunafish sandwich and her glass of ordinary wine.

Someday, some night, he would open the door and instead of the emptiness she would be inside with the glow of her smile, the glow that never seemed to come anymore except after deep crying and his eyes washed clean.

She looked something like the young woman who now stood by the stairs and seemed indifferent to whether she was chosen or not.

The other men let the stranger pass and they watched as he walked in and made his decision.

A madam came in between.

"Many lira."

"How many?"

"How many you have?"

"This many."

"You have no more?"

"No, it is all I have."

It was nothing to a hooker in Oakland but it was enough for the one by the stairs.

She was about the same age as Mary, the age of beauty queens and pinups, the age when a peasant woman becomes a mother.

She climbed the stairs ahead, the crease between her buttocks like the line he had always wanted, perfect and final.

She lay on the bed and pointed to her watch. She babbled something impatient. Co'mon, shove it in and be done with it.

She was annoyed by the long stare. Listen, buster, you pay to stick it in and that's all.

She flapped her arms in annoyance and the insides were dappled purple with needle marks. Co'mon now, for god's sake.

The hard-on softened and she wasn't going to raise it. Co'mon, if you can't I'm leaving.

The cock was full but not hard and yet she was warm and surprisingly wet and somehow it managed to slip inside.

Inside her needlemarks and her childhood in a gutter. Inside her future in a ghetto where she would beg for a bite of life and her skin would hang from her bones.

Inside the darkness of her bush that was like the darkness a child would have to go into whenever his mother told him to take the garbage to the basement.

He had never wanted to but his older brother would somehow always manage to forget, and he would have to carry it down the three flights and then open the door of the cellar and turn on the bulb that was never bright enough. Then he would tiptoe softly down the loose wooden steps so they would not creak and waken whatever was living in the darkness behind the grimy furnace, serpents or monsters or whatever was the opposite of what lived behind the altar in church, or were they both the same kind of darkness? He would tiptoe with his bag of garbage for the cans in the rear with almost the same motion he made when he tiptoed along the pew with his nickel for the candle. He would dump the garbage in the can as if it were an offering to a monster and he would stretch his arm as far as he could so no rat would jump on him and then he would turn and try not to run as if running would make something run after him, his breath held tight as he walked slowly past the furnace and the hissing flames that seemed to watch him like a huge animal in a cage. Finally at the stairs he would race up two at a time with something almost biting his heel as he escaped out the door.

Such was the terrible darkness of the cellar and yet one afternoon the landlord's granddaughter wanted to go into it.

She used to visit with her parents and she was a good playmate on rainy afternoons. She was very pretty as well and usually got her way. She wanted to go to the cellar and there by the sleeping dragon she wanted to play doctor and patient in the hiss of the flames. She lowered her panties and offered her buttocks like a golden grail, their heat and their power intensified by the very slight but pleasant odor of her feces that lingered from inside the exciting line.

She was the first one, the brazen little girl of the shadows, her mischievous eyes peeking over her shoulder at the little doctor who explored her buns, his hands eager and his cheeks flushed, her face burning into oblivion and forged under all those to come.

She stared at the ceiling while her client grew hard inside her and tried to plunge further.

He didn't want to come. He wanted to keep going and plunge deeper as if there were another entrance in the dark cellar of her secret, a hidden space in a deeper level where all monsters became friends and transformed into angels.

He wanted to stay inside her and kiss her and know her, her flesh at once both numb and warm, her beauty bruised and culled like a perfect apple mishandled and dropped too many times, the poor girl who could have been the great-granddaughter of the grandmother who died in the desert, her dark eyes and auburn hair at once both strange and kindred.

She was like one of his family who could lead him home again, she was like the girl in the dream whom the dreamer hugged as if she were his lost twin who grew up in another realm and waited for him to find her, his other half, his apples by the window upon waking and no one in the room but the cat meowing for food.

She hummed a tune to herself while she waited for him to come.

But he didn't want to come. He wanted to keep going as if somewhere inside her he could find the release and freedom like the stillness upon waking that morning when he looked through the window of the hostel by Saint Sophia, dawn very near and the sparrows just beginning to chirp, the dream and the darkness fading and through the line between sleep and waking those long mesmeric syllables wafting over the rooftops and flowing somewhere full of pain and ecstasy all together in an endless stream, the *la ilah ila 'llah* of slaughter and caterwaul and the muezzin like a circumsized Christian boy longing for his mother and enthralled by the Moslem chant he was forced to learn, the minaret like a phallus in the dawn and both the dawn and the prayer dissolving into the spears of light on the soft venus mound of a mosque that was once a church.

She waited.

She waited and didn't know if he had come or not, the old gumshoe who was taking such a long time finding her.

Did he come, did he reach his end?

There was no end as long as he kept wanting her. She was like the wanting itself and the endless need to keep on going, she never stopped being beautiful.

She was like the echo of old Ingres telling the young Degas to keep on drawing. "Draw lines, young man, don't stop making lines."

They kept coming and the old Degas still made them in his mind's eye when he sat in blindness with his hands in his lap and rode buses around Paris, as if by always moving he could keep death away. He never stopped, he was always horny, his blind craving a guide to a light, the dear father who never married or had kids, a young nurse at his deathbed and everyone in the room thinking he was gone when his hand suddenly grabbed her arm and turned it toward the window, his eyes struggling to catch the last play of light on her supple flesh.

She seemed neither flesh nor light but whatever it was that had no end, that kept growing into garbage for a hole in the dark, the self-seeding flowers of everyone's eyes.

She waited, she waited for the cock inside her to shrink and slip away, but the old rooster wanted to hang around and play with her nipples. He still had more to come.

She pushed herself up and pointed to the wallet on the table. She rubbed her fingers as if she were twirling an invisible thread. She would get as much out of him as she could but he showed her that his wallet was empty.

She washed her cunt and then wiped it clean for one more gesture he would never forget.

In the last glimpse of her she was sitting at a table in the corner of the hallway and eating ravenously from a heaping plate of shish-kebab and pilaf, a poor miserable girl who didn't know how beautiful she really was.

At the end of the lane outside the bordello a donkey was tied to a post and standing in the shade. He lowered his head as a hand reached out. There was nothing in the hand but he let himself be petted anyway. He twitched his ear and his breath was warm and earthy as he puffed through his hairy and cavernous nostrils.

Life Sciences

· It's time to go. I don't want to take the bus in the dark.
· I'll stay a while longer, I can walk home.
· I'll talk with you in the morning.
· If I'm still alive.
· If you're not alive you can tell me in my dreams.
· Listen to these two.
· They think they're funny.

- We are funny.
- Death is not funny.
- I can make it funny if I want to make it funny.
- I don't care what it is.
- I still got some life left. My passport made me three years older than I really am.
- When your time comes you can say your passport is wrong.
- Then she will have to pay all her pension back.
- I'll give it back. I'll give everything back. They can even have my yoghurt.
- Do you have any yoghurt-starter? My yoghurt is all worn out.
- I have fresh yoghurt at home. I'll tell my granddaughter to bring you some.
- Don't bother her, I'll come and get it.
- No, she's home tomorrow, there's no school.
- Is she back in school?
- Yes, she decided to go back.
- What is she studying?
- Life, she says she's studying life.
- What do you mean she's studying life?
- That's what she told me, she said she was studying life sciences.
- Is there any money in that kind of subject?
- There's money in everything.
- Not in raisins. There's no money in raisins anymore.
- You wait, in a few years there'll be money in raisins again too.

This book comes after two others, *Voyages,* 1971 (reprinted 1980, and *Wash Me On Home, Mama,* 1978. Each one has the same narrator at different stages in his life. In *Voyages* he is a young man trying to find both an identity and a way of living in a country where he feels alienated, all of which leads him to search for a father and a patrimony he feels he has lost. In *Wash Me On Home, Mama* he is a bit older and has become more concerned with the need for a family of his own. At this stage he takes on the collective voice of a commune in the late Sixties and the people there become parts of himself that he tries to integrate. In both books there is a female figure that is not quite developed, and as he tries to see her clearly in this new one he comes to a stage in his life where identity and family take on different meanings.

Like the narrator the author grew up between the Hudson River and the Hackensack marshland, the Watchung hills rolling in the west and the skyscrapers of Manhattan like a castle on the other shore.

And in this final space the author would like to acknowledge some friends and writers who are connected to the making of this book: Erich Neumann and Heinrich Zimmer, for all the gathering and sorting; Greg Hairabedian, Bob Ohannesian, and Ed Sahagian, for all the years of fraternity; John Ruhlman and Willy Smolak, for all the walks and meditations; Bill Belli, Hank Heifetz, and Jim Mohan, for all the waves under the bridge; Renate Victor, for all the sauerbraten and the Hershey Bar; and so many more for all the love and friendship no sentient being should be without, and finally, Bernie Spain and Dolly Tarquini, may their souls rest in peace.